GHOSTS
OF THE
PENNYRILE

Ghosts of the Pennyrile

A Collection of Short Ghost Stories

Rebecca Solomon

ISBN: 153721442X
ISBN-13: 978-1537214429

CONTENTS

AUTHOR'S NOTES

I would like to thank my editor, Will Overby, for being my sounding board and doing such a fine job of putting my books together. Thanks also to my friend Kay for listening and letting me know when something needs tweaking or doesn't work. Thanks to all of my readers for making my first book of ghost stories, Ghosts Along The Tradewater, such a success.

Pennyrile Forest State Resort Park in Dawson Springs, KY is one of my favorite places. It was the place I most looked forward to going when I was a child and later on, a teenager. Pennyrile is beloved by all who have hiked its trails, gone swimming or boating in its lake, picnicked on its grounds, camped or played golf there, regular or miniature. Many of my friends had their first summer jobs there.

Pennyrile has 15,331 acres of the most beautiful forest in Kentucky. Named for a little plant called Pennyroyal, which grows in the area, the park became a part of the Kentucky State Parks System in 1954. Before that, it had been under the supervision of the United States Department of Agriculture. In the 1930's a recreational tract of 300 acres was developed. The WPA (Works Progress Administration) built the rustic stone and wood lodge.

I decided the park is a perfect setting for ghost stories, with its wooded trails, hidden limestone nooks, and long history. I do want to point out that none of the stories in this book are "legends" or anything of the sort. Some of them are set in the surrounding region of rolling hills and woods. There have certainly been some strange happenings in this part of Kentucky and sometimes I have taken my inspiration from some of them. I have never heard of any part of the Park itself being haunted or having any strange happenings at all. These stories are fiction, and not intended to be taken as true, and no person living or dead is represented in any of them, with one exception.

In The Strange Playmate I briefly referred to John Peter Salling, a Kentucky explorer from 1742. The boy in the story claimed to be his son. I don't know if Salling even had a son, and the incidents the boy described never took place.

These stories are perfect if you like being just a little scared around your campfire or sitting on your lodge balcony overlooking the moonlit lake. Enjoy!

NIGHT CRAWLERS

"How about going fishing today?" Mike asked his friend Billy. They sat astride their old bikes at the edge of the Tradewater River, down by the mill dam.

"Yeah!" answered Billy. "We can dig some worms ourselves down by that old shack in the woods. They say there are big ones there."

The shack in question sat off the beaten path and hadn't been used in years. The boys didn't know who had built it, but had been warned away from it by their parents. Other kids said it was haunted. The concern of their parents seemed to be the dilapidated state of the floorboards and its leaning walls. The roof sagged in the middle and Mike's dad had said it could fall at any time.

"Just so we don't go in," said Mike. He had noticed when his dad had warned him that he didn't look him in the eye, but kind of looked sideways, like there was more to the story. It piqued his curiosity, of course, being a twelve year old boy and all.

"Well, the worms would be outside in the ground," answered Billy. "Duh."

Mike bristled. "I'll bet you would be afraid to go in."

Billy jumped off his bike and set it on the kickstand. Hands on hips, he narrowed his eyes. "I would not. What's to be afraid of? Except bringing the whole thing down on top of me."

"There is something about it, Billy. Ain't you noticed how grownups look when they talk about it?"

"Well, maybe." Billy rubbed a grubby hand along his shorts leg. "And I've heard older kids say they don't even use it for a make-out spot. It's just creepy."

Mike squinted into the sun. "But I'll bet there's some big night crawlers down there. We could catch a mess of bluegill or catfish for supper."

They grinned at each other. It would be fine as long as they didn't go in the shack. They took off down the dirt path towards the deep, dark woods.

Soon the path petered out, and they were riding through high grass and old leaves. The going was hard. "Let's leave our bikes here," said Billy.

They leaned them against a couple of trees and started walking. "Keep an eye out for a sharp stick to dig with," said Mike. "Man, I wish I'd-a brought Dad's shovel. Only I wouldna been able to carry it on the bike."

Billy nodded, carefully picking his way. Soon the woods had darkened and very little sunlight penetrated the trees and brush.

"Are you sure this is the right way?"

Mike said, "Yep, I've been down here before. Me and Steve Conway was down here last year. I saw some of the biggest night crawlers I've ever seen."

Billy looked sideways. Was Mike lying? He decided he would soon see for himself, anyway. "What are we gonna put 'em in?" he asked.

Mike scratched his blond head. "Don't know. Start looking for a can or something. Surely someone has thrown something down we can use."

There were scraps of junk; paper, cans, wire, and other things that had lost their usefulness and been tossed down by people walking through. Soon they came across a can that looked a little less bent than the others and that they thought would be big enough.

Suddenly Billy stopped. "There it is!" He pointed through the trees. The shack crouched ahead of them, dark and moldy. Its walls were covered in moss and lichen, as were the roof shingles, those that remained. A sagging door stood open. It was a creepy place, all right.

But the ground at their feet was nice and damp and strangely free of many leaves. They looked around and soon found some sticks they could use for digging, and set to work. They didn't notice that the birds had stopped singing. No sound of crickets or anything marred the silence.

They dug for a few minutes in the soft earth, and it yielded quite a few ordinary size earthworms. They dropped them into the can along with enough dirt to keep them happy so they wouldn't crawl out.

Mike wiped his sweaty forehead. "Dang. Where are the big ones, I wonder?"

"Maybe they live in the shack." Billy grinned.

"Or maybe they only come out at night, since they're night crawlers," answered Mike.

"Naw, I've seen night crawlers in the daytime down by the river, and even baked on the sidewalk."

About that time they heard a slithering in the leaves. Billy slowly turned his head. It had come from the direction of the shack. "Wh-what was that?" he whispered.

Mike also looked. There it was again. Like something sliding along at the edge of the rotting foundation.

They left their digging and crept toward the sound. "Look!" said Mike. "Look at that thing!"

Billy almost yelled. It was a night crawler about two feet long, big as a snake. But there was no mistaking that smooth rounded head for anything else. Its segmented body was about two inches thick. It raised its head and it seemed to the boys that it looked hungrily at them, with an intelligence or at least awareness not found in ordinary night crawlers.

Goosebumps stood up on their arms. "Geez," whispered Billy, as he looked at the creature, mesmerized. About that time it slithered into a crack in the foundation and was gone.

"Wow! That thing would catch a whale!" said Mike.

Billy looked at him with contempt. "There ain't no whales in the Tradewater."

"Course not, it was just a way of sayin' how big it was," said Mike.

The boys crept closer to the door of the shack. "Wonder if it's inside?" speculated Billy.

They craned their heads around the door facing, what was left of it. The shack groaned. A breeze had sprung up and ruffled their sweaty hair. It should have been a relief on the hot afternoon, but it made them more uneasy. Another sound reached them like the beams overhead were struggling to hold up the roof. "If it's in here, how are we gonna kill it?" asked Mike.

"Billy held up his stick, which was stout and very pointed on the end. "With this. And if stabbing it don't work, I guess we could beat it to death."

Mike cringed. He wasn't too keen on that idea. He didn't know his friend was so bloodthirsty.

They eased over the threshold. A sour, musty smell invaded their nostrils. Almost like some dirty animal. They saw old rags and leaves on the floor and in the corners. But surprisingly the thing that excited them most was that the debris on the floor teemed with life; night crawlers of all sizes, from little finger size to five or six inches long!

"Man! The jackpot!" exclaimed Mike. "Run get the can, Billy! We can dump them little 'uns out and put some of these in there!"

He didn't notice the dark shadow gliding around the wall behind them, between them and the door. They had forgotten all about the grownups' warnings about not going in the shack. When Billy turned to go out the door, he screamed. A dark swirl of leaves as tall as he was and something within that he couldn't quite see blocked his way to the door.

"You boys ain't gonna steal my babies, are you?" something whispered from within the vortex.

Mike and Billy stared, speechless. A miserable groan began in Mike's throat and was all he could manage. Billy stood frozen with fear and shock.

Finally a wavery face appeared in the swirl. It was of a very old man, wrinkled and ugly. It looked like it was made of dust. "My night crawlers are my children," it whispered. "When I died in this old shack, no one came to help me except them. They brought me bits of mushrooms and other things from the woods. They slept beside me and kept me warm as I passed over. I promised them no one would harm them, and that they would grow unmolested. And they have. "

The giant worm they had seen outside slithered against their legs. That's when they started screaming, totally panicked, and ran straight through the swirl of leaves, encountering nothing solid, but feeling a chill all the way through their bodies. They did not stop until they got back to their bicycles in the woods where they had left them.

Somehow they moved on to several outside activities that summer, including fishing. But digging their own worms had lost its appeal. The ones from the bait shop would do just fine.

SCHOOL DAYS

Wyatt sat in a wooden chair in the center of the old schoolhouse. Dust motes floated in the sunbeams that filtered through the grimy windows and cracks in the wall. He looked around at the buildup of dirt and debris on the floor and sighed. So many memories.

The old wood burning stove still sat in the corner, looking like it was just waiting for someone to light a fire inside to warm up the children who came to learn inside these walls sixty years ago. Wyatt had been one of those kids. He was now 70 years old and his body was wearing out. Arthritis had nearly crippled him, to the point where he walked with a cane all the time now. He recalled the smell of wet wool as kids stood around the fire, trying to dry their mittens after coming in from the rain or snow outside; the hiss of the ashes when new wood was added and the leaping of the flames. Then Miss Morris would close the top and slide the damper over so the fire could get enough air.

He recalled many of his old schoolmates, now long in their graves. What he wouldn't give to see some of them again! Their teacher, Miss Morris, had been young and pretty. She had married a local farmer soon after starting to teach at the school. Of course, she was gone, too now, having been trampled by one of the farmer's pigs a few years after they were married. The farmer had never remarried, and remained on his farm until he died, but he got rid of all the hogs and started raising cattle and soybeans.

Wyatt closed his eyes. He saw it all in his mind's eye. Little Maureen O'Malley, made fun of because of her Irish accent and her poor immigrant family. He was ashamed that he had been one of her tormentors. And Tom Siegel, who had a withered arm. He wanted so badly to play baseball with the other boys, but they would never let him, even though he insisted he could catch the ball in one hand. Wyatt hadn't thought much about him at the time, in fact, had ignored him, if truth be told. Wyatt's family was not rich, but they had fertile fields and plenty to eat. Wyatt and his brother Will were both healthy.

He must have dozed off, because he began to see the parade of kids who were handicapped or less fortunate in some way, not the fond and sweet memories he had meant to dwell on. A piece of wood dropped inside the stove, and awakened him. He was shocked to see the schoolhouse as it was when he attended it all those years ago. The wooden floor was swept clean and the stove was aglow through the two small holes in the damper. He was at his old desk, third from the front in the left hand row if you were looking from the front to the back of the rows of desks.

Wyatt stared all around him at the children at their desks. But some were missing. His pal Gary, who was one of the best short stops in their baseball games, was not in the room. Neither were the kids whose parents were well off and had nothing of note about which to be teased and tormented. It was just the ones with some kind of anomaly, a handicap, scar, limp, speech impediment, or just were downright poor that sat there, all looking at him with accusing eyes.

And their eyes! They were glowing with malice. Wyatt now recognized that he was actually a bully in school. Uncomfortably, he remembered the times he had made faces and laughed at kids, and even tripped them on the playground. Thinking nothing of it at the time, it had slipped from his memory over the years. He could feel his heart starting to pound. Suddenly he was ashamed. As an adult, he realized that kids could not help these things that happened to them. They had no control, just as he had no control over the arthritis that made his days miserable.

"I'm sorry," he whispered. "So, so sorry. But I was just a kid!"

Maureen stood up, in her ragged dress. "Sorry don't make any difference now," she said, and he noticed that her teeth were razor sharp. "Even a kid should know better than to do the things you did."

Wyatt turned red, and nodded. "You're right! They should."

Lem Smith stood up, towering over the whole group. He was always tall for his age, and not that bright at his books, which earned him the name of Lem the Dummy. "You don't know how I struggled with my lessons," Lem said. "But no one offered to help me. You were the main one who started called me a dummy and laughing at me. I ended up in the Army, where I didn't need so much book learning. I got killed in the war. Sacrificed my life so people like you could have a comfortable life. But I would have liked to have married and had a family. But it won't ever happen now."

Wyatt nodded. "Thank you for your service," was all he could think of to say. He was embarrassed to feel tears on his cheeks.

Lem grinned with very sharp teeth, like the others. "That's not enough," he said.

One by one they stood and told him how his treatment of them made them feel, and in some cases stole their self confidence so that they never went as far in life as they had hoped they could have. There were ten in all who faced him and told him their stories.

Linda Lou Marks, a little girl who had been burned badly when she dropped a lantern and it caught her dress on fire, said, "And now you must pay." Her scarred face was shiny in the glowing light from the stove. He remembered laughing at her.

Wyatt was almost grateful when they fell on him, their sharp teeth biting and gnashing.

THE WELL

"Now, don't you kids fool around that old home place up the road. You could get hurt," warned my grandma.

My brother Ned, my sister Iris, and I were spending a week on the farm during our summer vacation. I'm Alice, and Iris and I are just a year apart. We were ten and nine respectively that summer, and Ned was twelve. We always looked forward to time at Grandma and Grandpa's. We spent our days fishing in the Tradewater River when one of the grownups could go with us, or searching the plowed fields for arrowheads. There were plenty of those in those days, for the Indians camped right there by the river a long time ago.

Sometimes we rode the horse, Tony, without a saddle. He was so gentle he never tried to buck us off or anything. As we grew, we were allowed to ride Tony up the road to the Slough (pronounced "slew") Bridge and back, which was about a mile. Grandpa insisted only two of us rode on the horse at one time, with the other one

12

leading him by his bridle. By taking turns, we were able to go the mile there and the mile back without anyone getting too tired.

On this day, we had decided to go to this old home place up the road where a family used to live, but had moved away years ago. The place was overgrown with weeds and blackberry brambles. This last was what drew us on this hot July day. We had seen the luscious berries from the road when we rode Tony last.

"But Grandma, we want to pick some blackberries, "said Ned. " We thought you might bake us a blackberry cobbler. Wouldn't that be good after supper?"

"Yes, Grandma, that's all we want to do. We won't go out of sight of the road," I chimed in.

Grandma looked like she was trying to make up her mind. But she loved to bake, so she reluctantly agreed. "Now, make sure you can see the road, and don't go any further than that. You should be able to get enough." She got us a tin bucket, and off we went.

The old house was gone, and only the foundation remained. It was not set back very far from the road, and the blackberries were all around in what used to be the yard. We set out happily picking, and eating almost as many as we picked. Ned was ahead of us girls. Suddenly we heard him say, "Oh!"

We pushed our way through the weeds to find him standing at the side of an old well, where a rusty chain held an old bucket from a pulley. It was very hot, and I felt a trickle of sweat down my back. The air felt heavy. Not a breeze stirred.

I opened my mouth to say we were not supposed to be so far

from the road. But I never said anything, for we all heard a small voice say, "Help me." I drew in a quick breath. Iris stood with her mouth open. Ned was leaning over the well, looking inside.

For some reason, I didn't want to look. He kept leaning further and further, and even though the well surround was waist high, he lost his balance and before I could move, fell in. I heard him scream all the way down and I yelled to Iris to run as fast as she could to get Grandpa.

She took off down the road. I rushed to the side of the well. Ned was bobbing in the water, barely holding onto a stone that was sticking out from the wall. "Help, help!" He cried.

"Hold on, Ned, Iris has gone to get Grandpa! Are you hurt?"

He finally calmed a little and looked up at me. "I-I don't think so. But the child...the child..."

"What child?" I called down to him. His face looking up at me was white as a sheet.

"The child in the well...oh, she is pulling on my legs!"

My hair stood on end. "There's no one there but you, Ned! Just hold on!"

I saw his hand slip almost off of the stone. He seemed to be struggling to stay above the water.

Suddenly I saw something white beside him in the water. It was just under the surface, wavering and undulating in the disturbed water.

Ned began to cry in earnest. "Jesus, save me! I'm going to drown!"

"No, you're not!" I was more frightened than I had ever been. For I could swear I could see a little girl's pale face under the surface of the water next to Ned.

Then I heard heavy running footsteps behind me. I turned and saw that it was Grandpa and he had brought a big coil of rope he kept hanging in the barn.

He ran to the side of the well, and called down to Ned. "Catch the rope, son, and I'll pull you out!"

He wrapped the rope around his waist and tied it, then quickly dropped it down to Ned. Then his mouth dropped open and his eyes bugged out. "Oh, my gracious goodness," he whispered.

Ned grabbed onto the rope and wrapped the end around his arm. Soon Grandpa began to pull. I could tell he was having a hard time. Iris and I grabbed the rope in front of him and added our weight to it. Ned did not weigh 80 pounds soaking wet. But it felt like a much larger weight was on the rope. Suddenly the weight lessened, and Ned came up quickly. Grandpa grabbed him and hauled him over the edge.

Again we heard the little voice…"Help me."

I started to the well, but Iris grabbed my dress. Grandpa took my arm, and with one arm around Ned, and the other on mine, he said, "Let's get out of here." We were all shivering, but especially Ned. I did think to pick up the blackberry bucket, which was nearly full. But somehow I was not as interested in blackberry cobbler as I had been.

Grandma saw us coming. Grandpa had not even had time to tell her what was going on. She rushed down the front porch steps and hustled Ned into the house as Grandpa told her what happened. "I had heard about it, but never seen it," he said.

He proceeded to tell us that the family that had moved away from the home place had had a little girl, seven years old. She had fallen into the well and drowned. People had said the place was haunted; Grandma and Grandpa had never believed in "haints," as we call them in the South. But they do now. And Ned's hair had turned completely white, and stayed that way the rest of his life. So if the grownups tell you to stay away from a place, you'd better listen.

THE GHOST IN THE LAKE

Thunder rumbled across Pennyrile Lake and Lodge. A wind sprung up, and a shaft of lightning drove hikers and beachgoers to the lodge building. The leaves on the trees blew backward, some of them carried to the ground as the rain began to pour down.

Visibility became poor among the trees and on the trails around the lake. People with tents in the camping area sought cover in their neighbors' more substantial campers, where the smell of coffee drifted out on the air. They settled in to drink coffee and visit as the storm intensified and fog rolled in.

Jeremy and I were halfway around the lake when the storm blew up. Our backpacks became heavier as we hurried along, having turned around to start back to the lodge. Our way lay across the dam at the end of the lake, which would take us up to the back of the lodge. But we figured it would be easier than continuing in the woods.

"Slow down!" I called to Jeremy, as he trotted in front of me. "I can't keep up with you."

"Sorry," he said, looking back. "I forget how short your legs are."

When we came out onto the blacktop next to the cottages on the shore across from the lodge, it was slick. My feet flew out from under me, and I fell on my backpack, which probably saved me from breaking bones. Jeremy heard me and turned around to help me up.

"Are you okay?"

"Yes, just my pride is hurt," I said. "I'm also soaked to the skin."

"Well, I am, too. Let's just get on to our room in the lodge and get into some dry clothes. Some hot chocolate from Clifty Creek Restaurant sounds good about now."

I agreed and we started down the steps onto the dam. The fog was so thick by now we could hardly see one foot in front of the other. I looked over the railing on the lake side along the top of the dam. I could see the water at the bottom, strangely enough. It was dimpled with the hard raindrops.

Suddenly something broke the surface of the water. It was pale and long. "Oh, my gosh!" I was shocked to see an arm and hand emerging from the depths.

"What?" Jeremy came over to stand beside me. About that time, lightning lit up the sky. I grabbed onto him and we held each other until it quietened down.

"I saw something in the water!" I was shaking.

He looked over the side. "You can't even see the water. The fog is too thick."

"N-no, it wasn't a minute ago. Jeremy, it was someone's arm!"

He looked strangely at me. "Impossible. It's the fog playing tricks." He grabbed my hand and started pulling me along. About that time, a long roll of thunder preceded another big flash of lightning.

We instinctively squatted down, to make ourselves a smaller target. When it had passed, we looked over the side again. This time a wavery face appeared, seemingly smiling and then grimacing. It was surely a trick of the water. This time Jeremy saw it, too.

"Holy Moly!" His mouth dropped open. "We need to get up to the lodge and get help."

I had a very creepy feeling wash over me. "Somehow I think this person is beyond help," I whispered. But he had already started across the rest of the dam, and I hurriedly followed.

I couldn't help looking over my shoulder. When I did, I saw the person looking over the railing at me. I was convinced that it was no living being. It looked female, long dripping hair down its back. Its eyes were deep black and round. I screamed and ran after Jeremy.

The rain had stopped and the fog had started to lift when we finally reached the lodge. Luckily one of the back doors to the big gathering room was open. We rushed around the corner to the front desk.

I was so out of breath and so upset by what I had seen, I let Jeremy do the talking.

"There is a body in the lake by the dam!" he said. "My wife and I saw it. Call 911."

I kept quiet about seeing it at the top of the dam. I didn't want people to think I was crazy. But I was certain they wouldn't find anything.

I was right. We heard the sirens on the road to the dam, and walked back down. "We're going to have to drag the lake," I heard one of the EMTs say to another rescue person. "I can't see anything down there. I doubt if they are still alive."

The other guy nodded and went back to the ambulance and I saw him pick up his radio mic.

They drug the lake the next day and the day after that. No body turned up. I was in the gathering room by the fireplace when the rescue operators came in and went to the front desk. One of the dining room waitresses came and sat by the fire on her break while they were talking to the desk clerk.

"I knew they wouldn't find anything," she said quietly to me. "I've been here for twenty years and this has happened once before that I know of. It was several years ago."

"Tell me about it, please." I said. Jeremy had come over by then and he sat down with us to listen to her story.

"You may know that Pennyrile State Park was developed in the 1930's by the Works Progress Administration."

We nodded. We had looked up the history of the park. Many workers had come from all over, taking advantage of the President's work projects after the stock market crash of 1929 when there was not much work available otherwise.

"Well, there was a man that was killed while they were building that dam. He was buried under the tons of rock and concrete and his body was never found. When someone went to inform his wife of his death she went crazy. Went down to that dam crying and screaming and threw herself over the edge before anyone could stop her. You know how the dam slopes outward at the bottom. Well, she hit the bottom of the dam and was instantly killed. Since then, every now and then, someone sees her in the water or climbing up the side of the dam. They say she is still looking for his body. I saw her one time, and hope to never see her again."

I shivered. Jeremy's mouth was hanging open.

"That is just what I saw!" I exclaimed. "How horrible! I knew it was a ghost as soon as I saw her looking at me over the side. No one who was drowning would have had the strength to climb up the side like that."

"I didn't say that to the rescue personnel, of course," she said. "The manager has seen it, too, but he doesn't want us to talk about it, for good reason. It might be bad for business. And most people don't believe in ghosts and would think we were a bunch of lunatics."

I nodded. At least I knew we had actually seen something. It's not something you go around telling. But I have never gone across the dam on a rainy day again.

THE OLD MILL DAM GHOST

There are places where the veil between past and present is very thin. Dawson Springs has some places like that. A local ghost hunter I was acquainted with a few years ago said that I would be surprised at how many haunted places there were in Dawson Springs and the Tradewater region. I have experienced strange feelings and a reluctance to go into or close to some places because of an uneasiness I could not name. The old Mill Dam on the river is one such place.

Around the turn of the century the Dawson Milling Company was operating six days a week, grinding the corn brought in by local farmers by horse and mule wagon. It was a good living for the family that operated the mill. I don't recall their names now; in fact, I don't know that I ever knew their names. But they left an impression on the place that was so important to so many.

My friend Barry and I liked to go fishing by the old mill dam in the 1960's. The mill building itself was long gone, of course, but the rushing water was still there. We had caught quite a few fish there. But we also had an eerie experience. One late May afternoon we were happily fishing and started hearing a loud grinding noise behind us, right where the mill once stood. It sounded as if the ground and the rocks themselves were moving against each other. When we turned around to look it stopped.

A feeling of dread came over us. I laid my pole down and stood up, staring at the site of the mill. The sun was starting to go down and it was getting about time for us to leave. The air temperature felt like it had dropped about ten degrees. "Lacy? What was that?" whispered Barry.

"I don't know," I answered. But everything felt different. I can't explain how, exactly. I felt an oppression come over me to the point that I felt like I was going to faint.

We stared at the spot intently. Then the grinding noise came again, along with the most awful scream we had ever heard. We about jumped out of our skins.

"Bobcat," I said, not believing it for an instant.

Barry nodded. "Yeah, that's what it must have been." The only problem with that was that it was coming from right in front of us and there was nothing there.

I noticed that all sound became muffled, even the water rushing over the mill dam. No whippoorwills called, as they were wont to do in the evening. Suddenly it seemed as if the trees around were thicker and darker. Night was drawing in a lot quicker than we had realized. But still we stood rooted to the spot.

An unearthly moan split the air. It was coming from right where the giant millstones used to sit. Then the grinding noise again. A form began to appear, square and large. And before our eyes, the old mill rose again, dark clapboards and two stories, just like it was in its heyday.

By this time I was gripping Barry's hand and we were shaking all over. The building was not clear, but rather like we were looking at it through a haze. Then, as quickly as it came, it began to dissipate.

Suddenly the air felt lighter, the water was louder, and I noticed the chill in the air was gone. We looked at each other. We both picked up our poles and tackle boxes and our container of bluegill and hightailed it for home.

We lived next door to each other. When we reached home I said, "Are you going to tell anybody?"

"I would like to," said Barry. "But the other kids will think we're crazy."

"I know," I said. "My grandma knows everything about this town and the river. She never laughs at me no matter what. We can tell her."

So we went inside where Mom was getting the table set for supper, gave her the bluegill to put in the refrigerator, and went in search of my grandma. I found her on the front porch mending one of her dresses.

She hugged me. "Catch any fish?" she asked, smiling. "Barry, you'll stay for supper."

He nodded. She always just told us what we were going to do. He was just like family and didn't need to be invited.

"Yes, but Grandma, something happened down there. I'm still not sure what. Maybe you will know." So I told her the whole story and when I was finished, she was very quiet, and sat looking at the floor like she was thinking.

"I don't like to scare kids," she began. "But back years ago when the mill was operating in the late 1800's, they say that one of the mill workers had an accident. It was late in the day and his job was to put the corn on the bottom millstone and then the top one would come down and grind it into cornmeal. Somehow he tripped and fell under the top stone as it was coming down; too late for the operator to stop it. It ground him into pulp. There was nothing left but blood and a little flesh. Not enough to even bury. And now they say that his ghost haunts the place because he never got a proper burial and can't be at peace."

My eyes were about to bug out of my head. Barry never said a word. I couldn't even hear him breathing.

"I never believed it," Grandma went on. "I never believed in ghosts. So this is kind of a shock to me, too. I guess it has to be the right time of day for it to appear. There's a lot of strange things." She shook her head. "I'm not too old to find out something new."

Barry said, "I didn't want to find that out."

Grandma reached over and patted him on the arm. "Well, you don't have to be afraid of things like that. They are just shadows and impressions of things past. They can't hurt you."

"Well, unless they cause you to die of fright," I chimed in.

"But you didn't," she said, smiling. "Let's go to the kitchen and see if we can help your mother."

I tugged on her sleeve. "Grandma, I have an idea. Why don't we make some kind of a marker for the man who was ground up? So he would be remembered. I mean, in a good way. Maybe then he would stop haunting the place."

She looked down at me. "I think that's a wonderful idea."

The next day we found a stone marker in a catalog that didn't cost very much. It was made for pets, but they would put whatever name on it you wanted. I didn't figure the "miller" (which was what I thought of him as), would mind. Barry and I pooled our allowances we had saved up and sent off for it. A few days later it arrived in the mail.

Grandma, Mother, Barry, his mother, and I all went down to the mill dam one morning when the sun was out and the birds were singing. The day would be hot later, but now there was a pleasant warm breeze playing through the trees.

I ceremoniously took the stone marker out and we dug out a little flat place with a small shovel we had brought along. We laid it in and lined it with river stones. We had guessed at the date of his death, and of course we didn't know his name. "God knows who he is," I said, and they all agreed.

On the stone, we had had inscribed:

Miller

Gone but not forgotten

1850

No one to my knowledge has ever experienced the ghostly appearances again.

THE GHOSTLY DANCERS

I hurried up the South Main Street hill. A bunch of us teens were going to meet at Donna's house to watch the Beatles on the Ed Sullivan show. It was colder than heck. I pulled my scarf tighter around my neck and shoved my gloved hands into my coat pockets.

We had looked forward to this show all week. I didn't want to be late. I had just passed the new post office. It was close to dark and the street was empty. I saw one lone car go past toward the center of town. I shivered. I was looking down at the sidewalk and became aware of someone in front of me.

Raising my head, I saw the back of a lady in a long dress and coat. She was wearing a fanciful hat with lots of feathers. Her companion beside her was a man in a sort of top hat. His coat was below his knees and divided into tails in the back. Something about them made the hair on the back of my neck rise.

They bent their heads close together, talking as they walked.

Suddenly I heard strains of waltz music, like it was really far away. I stopped and held my breath. Where could it be coming from? It was probably someone's television set. But all the houses nearby looked dark and shuttered, doors and windows closed tight against the winter chill.

The couple passed the big white house on the corner that I had heard was the first to get electric lights in the community. There was one more house and then the building that used to house the Ford Garage where my dad had worked when I was small. After that, an empty lot.

There were a couple of old steps leading into the lot. It was where the old H&H Pavilion had stood back in the 1890's. I was surprised to see them go up the steps, the lady holding up her skirt with one hand, her other one wrapped around the man's arm. Then they just disappeared. The music continued to play, just loud enough that my ear could pick it up by straining and being very still.

I really had a creepy feeling. I didn't want to walk by there. But if I didn't I was going to miss the Beatles! I know, I thought, I'll just look down and hurry on past. In fact, I can cross the street.

It seemed as I crossed the street, the air got colder and a sharp breeze sprang up, scented with leaves and coal smoke from the many chimneys in town. Lots of people still used coal stoves to heat their houses. I had meant to rush on up the street, but the music got a little louder, and I could really make it out now.

There was a glow coming from the empty lot. I couldn't help

but look. I saw a building with open sides, and people were milling about inside, some dancing and some standing around the banisters at the edge. The whole place was lit up by bulbs that hung from the ceiling. Though it was cold, the ladies inside had bare shoulders and sweeping gowns that swirled as they turned about the dance floor. I could hear people laughing and talking. I couldn't tell which couple was the one I saw in front of me on the street. I was so amazed and frightened that I was rooted to the spot.

I noticed I could see through them! I now could tell that the waltz they were playing was The Blue Danube by Strauss. The orchestra was very hazy because it was at the other end of the pavilion. I stood mesmerized as the dancers dipped and twirled. It was so beautiful I forgot to be frightened.

I don't know how long I stood there. At last the scene began to fade and after a few minutes of getting dimmer and dimmer, it disappeared. A last haunting strain of the waltz floated over the frosted air. Then darkness prevailed and all was still. The lot was empty once again.

I barely made it to Donna's just as the Ed Sullivan show was coming on. I was bursting to tell the other girls what I had seen, but I would have to wait until after the Beatles. I knew that no matter how good they were going to be, I would treasure the memory of the ghostly dancers in the old pavilion. I think of them now every time I pass the old steps into the empty lot on South Main. I believe that just as horrible things leave a lasting memory and impression on a place, happy times can as well.

PHOTOGRAPHS

WPA workers building the lodge at Pennyrile Forest State Resort Park, ca. 1937-38. (Used by permission.)

Building the dam, ca. 1937-38. (Used by permission.)

Pennyrile Dam before its completion. (Used by permission.)

Fisherman's Rock with diving platform in the background, ca. 1960s. (Used by permission.)

Pennyrile Beach, ca. early 1970s. (Used by permission.)

Pennyrile Lodge in the fall, present day. (Photo by the author.)

Beautiful Pennyrile Lake. (Photo by the author.)

Scarecrow that was the inspiration for the story "The Scarecrow."
(Photo by the author, by permission of Billy Johnson.)

THE MOONLIGHT DIVE

"Let's go down to Pennyrile Beach tonight," suggested Bryce during fourth period study hall on Friday. "The moon is supposed to be full. It'll be fun!"

Annie and I agreed. "I don't have much homework, at least so far," I whispered. I kept my voice low because Mr. Black was looking at our table with a frown.

Annie leaned over and said, "Don't look now but Black is staring over here."

We all opened our books and began to read. I did have a report I was supposed to be working on. But it was hard to concentrate, as I was thinking about Pennyrile State Resort Park, our favorite place in the whole world. We had all been there many times through our growing up years, swimming, picnicking, fishing, and hiking with our families and friends.

I loved the beach best of all. It was where all the teens gathered in the summer and swam, sunned themselves, and flirted. Many a romance started and ended on that beach. Soldiers from nearby Fort Campbell also came to the park in the summer. They seemed so grownup and romantic compared to the pimply boys we all knew from school. I was forbidden by my dad to talk to them, but I enjoyed looking, anyway.

It was now the end of May of our junior year and only a few more days left of school. Already the days had grown hot and the nights were pleasant. It would be a perfect night on the beach. If only my parents would let me go. Surely they would, since Bryce and Annie were going. My mom and dad liked both of them and knew their parents well. They were twins and lived two houses down from me.

Later at our lockers, Bryce nudged me with his elbow. "They say that on a full moon night, there are monsters in the lake." He was laughing.

"Yeah, sure there are," I said. "Can't wait to see 'em." Trying to get him back, I whispered in my best Boris Karloff voice, "I do know that there are snakes in the lake." I knew he was terrified of snakes, though he tried to hide it.

"Yeah, but they don't come to the beach area," he said.

"Maybe not," I grinned.

"We'll swing by and pick you up about eight, Linda," said Annie. She had gotten her driver's license just a few weeks ago. Bryce still had not. It was a sore spot with him. But he had flunked the test and been sent home to study the manual for another couple of weeks.

"Are you sure you can get the car?" I asked.

"I'm pretty sure, if I say we're going to the library," she said, and winked at me.

Annie was the wild one. She was always the one who wanted to do something we weren't supposed to do, or go just beyond what we were comfortable with. I admired her in a way, but she scared me sometimes, too.

That night they drove up in front of my house right on time. Annie had her dad's second car, a maroon Oldsmobile. I didn't know the year, I just knew it was not a cool car. But no way was he going to let her have the new Rav 4.

"If we scrootch down in the seat, no one will see us," joked Bryce. Annie punched him on the arm.

I grinned. "Sounds like a plan," I said.

Annie made a face at me. "How would you two just like to call it all off?" she said, pretending to be mad.

"Then these peanut butter cookies my mom made would just go to waste," I said. "Oh, wait; I could eat all of them myself."

As we sped off down the street we were all laughing.

About fifteen minutes later, we were carrying our picnic cooler and blankets down through the dark woods to the beach. There was a nice, wide blacktop path from the parking area, and since the moon was up, we had no trouble seeing the way. It was just dark enough to be pleasantly spooky.

As we neared the steps down to the beach, we could see the moon sparkling on the water. Annie quickly spread our blankets out and we set the cooler by them. The sand was pleasantly cool. I buried my toes in it and sighed. "This is the life," I said.

The beach, pale in the moonlight, stretched away on either side and met the cliff several hundred yards to the left of where we sat. To our right and further down was the boat dock where people rented paddle boats and rowboats for fishing. No one else was on the beach and we built a small fire. It was prohibited, but it seemed so quiet that we didn't figure anyone would even know about it. The lodge was way on the other end of the lake.

Annie and Bryce pulled out hot dogs, buns, and mustard, and I had brought Cokes and the cookies my mom had made. We had already cut our sticks and brought them with us and now we put our dogs on and held them over the fire.

"Boy, that smells good," said Bryce as he turned his dogs over and over. "Did anyone bring marshmallows?"

"No!" I said. "I wish I'd thought of that; I love roasted marsh-mallows!"

"Me, too," said Annie.

He shrugged and went on turning the hot dogs over the fire.

The full moon created a silver path of light across the lake. We could hear the slight ripples in the breeze. It was a beautiful sight.

Then I heard something across the lake, thrashing around in the bushes and trees at the top of the cliff. The lake was not very large and sound carried across the water. We all looked over towards the cliffs and the large rocks below where signs warned people not to dive off into the water there. It was called Fisherman's Rock. The water was not as deep there as it looked. However some people had been known to dive there anyway. It was nice and deep just beyond the rocks, but you had to know how far out to jump.

"Look," Annie pointed out. "Someone's over there."

"I hope we're not in trouble for having a fire," Bryce said.

"I see shadows on top of the rocks," I said quietly. "Who would be silly enough to climb around up there at night? I know people dive over there even though they aren't supposed to. But at night?"

The sound of guys laughing came to us over the lake, with that echo quality that voices have across a body of water. We could barely see them moving around on the rocks, coming up to the edge and then backing away as if they had changed their minds. There were three or four of them. It was hard to tell exactly, as they were in the shadow of the trees.

Then we watched as a man walked out onto the rock nearest the lake. Only he looked strange; he was all white, bathing trunks and all. The other shadows had disappeared.

"Where did they all go?" I said.

Bryce and Annie didn't answer, because just then we saw him clasp his stretched out hands together and dive off into the water. But there was no splash, no noise at all. The water was undisturbed. We waited, but he didn't surface.

We looked at each other. I shivered in spite of the fire. Something was not right. We quickly kicked sand over the fire and just left everything and made for the car. "We've got to get to the lodge and get help," Bryce said.

Annie sped around the curvy road. Luckily the lodge wasn't far. The man at the front desk looked up in alarm as we fell in the front door. We must have looked like we were frightened to death, because he hurried around the counter. "What's wrong?" he asked, taking Annie by the arm and leading her to a nearby chair.

"Someone just dived off the rocks in the lake! And he was all white, and he didn't come up, and you need to get help!" I managed to stammer out.

"All white, you say?" the man said, and we all nodded.

"It was the weirdest thing I ever saw. He didn't even make a splash," said Annie.

The man shook his head. "What you saw is not common, but not unheard of, either," he said. "A few years ago, some soldiers were up there and one of them dove off and didn't jump far enough out, being unfamiliar with the lake and the rocks. He hit a rock on the bottom and broke his neck. He died instantly. Since then, every once in awhile, he has been seen repeating that fatal dive. I feel almost certain that was what you saw. But just in case, I'll call the state police and an ambulance."

Of course, they never found anything at all. We were so creeped out we never even went back for our cooler. The park ranger brought it up to the lodge and I went out the next weekend and picked it up.

We asked about the darker shadows that seemed to be people. "Some of the soldier's friends were with him, and they can be seen in the background, "the ranger answered.

"I'm through with night picnics on the beach," I said. Bryce and Annie agreed.

WILL O' THE WISP

Clouds were scudding past the moon over Pennyrile Lake. The beach was deserted, the boat dock empty except for the bobbing paddle boats on their chains. A sighing breeze wafted through the pines, oaks, and maples that surrounded the gleaming body of water. The swimmers, hikers, and picnickers had gone home for the day, or to their cozy rooms in Pennyrile Lodge.

Nineteen year old Clay Hunter gave one last tug on the lock that held the chains on the paddleboats. His day of work was over. He was a little late leaving, as he had taken his time over his paperwork, carefully tallying up the day's take from renting the boats. He was enjoying his summer job.   It was a warm June night. He paused to listen to voices carrying from the cabins on the other side of the lake. He could make out the glow of campfires and grills as people cooked their simple meals and enjoyed the camaraderie that was to be found only in the outdoors.

He was reluctant to leave. The lake was inviting. It would be so nice and quiet out there with no other boaters or noise, just the faint laughter from the shore. There was an old rowboat tied to the dock that the park manager and employees used sometimes to do a little fishing in their off hours. Clay smiled and headed toward it after he had locked up the rental office.

He pulled out his cell phone and called his mom to let her know he wouldn't be home for dinner, that he was going out on the lake to try to catch a fish or two. He really didn't plan on fishing, but didn't want her asking questions such as why he would want to row out there just to sit on the water. She was always asking questions. Sometimes a guy just wanted to be alone with his thoughts. She didn't seem to understand that.

He slid the boat into the water, jumped in and lined up the oars in their locks, and started rowing. Pennyrile was one of those places that had a kind of magic about it; it just made him happy to be there. The only other place that seemed to rest under a dome of peace like that was his grandfather's farm. The world just seemed to melt away.

The boat glided smoothly, creating little ripples as it sliced through the water under the moon. Clay was headed towards the other end of the lake where hundreds of lily pads floated in the water. He could hear the boom of bullfrogs and the shriller croak of smaller frogs that lived in the lily pads. The unique pine scent that was Pennyrile drifted into his nose and he breathed deeply.

He glanced toward the shore and saw something moving through the trees in the forest, glimmering and fading in and out.

He did a double take. It seemed to be moving in the same direction he was. He had heard of will o'the wisps, the glowing gases from rotting logs and vegetation that could sometimes be seen in the woods at night. That must be what it was. He turned back to his rowing and could see the lily pads up ahead.

He could no longer hear sounds from the cabins and campers. It was just the breeze and the sloshing water and the frogs. The hoot of an owl startled him a little bit and he looked toward the shore. The will o'the wisp, or whatever it was, was nearer the lake and still moving. It was about the size of a person, much higher up than a rotting log. How weird, was his thought as the figure became clearer. It was like someone standing on the edge of the lake, just looking at him.

"Who's there?" he called out, hating the tremor in his voice.

The figure raised its arms and he saw that it had taken the shape of a young woman with long flowing hair. He could not really make out a face, but suddenly he heard the most beautiful singing he had ever heard. It seemed to touch his soul deep down inside. It was like it was calling him. The melody was haunting, sounding both strange and familiar. It reminded him of a hymn or a ballad he might have heard in years past.

Clay turned the boat toward the shore as the figure beckoned him. The girl (or whatever it was) slowly stepped down into the water. "Be careful, it's deep there!" shouted Clay. She ignored him and walked right down until she disappeared underneath the lake and the lily pads.

He stood up in the boat, thoroughly spooked now. The singing started again, this time nearer. He turned toward it quickly, rocking the boat and almost falling into the water. She had swum out to him and was looking at him from the water with her hands on the side of the boat. Her hands were long and white, longer than they should be.

As he took this in, he looked at her face and saw a strange kind of beauty, but there was something off about it. Her eyes were an odd almond shape, and she had a very wide mouth. Even though she was singing, her mouth did not open. The air seemed to vibrate with her humming. And the glow that surrounded her was almost blinding.

Clay stood paralyzed as she began to climb into the boat. He was too frightened to even offer her his hand. Her garments were thin and flowing, dripping water. She got one foot over the side easily enough. With horror, he saw that it was webbed like a frog's. He screamed as her long tongue snaked out and buried itself in his chest. Then the acid in her proboscis began to dissolve the soft tissues. His last coherent thought was that his organs were being pulled out of his body. She lay beside him after he fell and fed until there was nothing left. Then she slid over the side of the boat and back into the lake, leaving a trail of slime.

THE SCARECROW

"The dang birds are eating almost every seed I get in the ground," Mack complained. "I'm going to have to put up a scarecrow. Don't know if it'll do any good."

Mack was a third generation farmer on his family's bottom land next to the Tradewater River. His daddy had grown corn and cattle. His granddaddy had grown tobacco and sheep. Mack had sold his tobacco base and planted corn and soybeans, and also raised a few head of cattle. His crops did well most years. But this was a particularly bad year for birds; mostly blackbirds and crows.

"Sally Ann," he called as he clomped up on the front porch of his farmhouse. His wife came from the kitchen, wiping her hands on a towel.

"What's wrong?" she asked, a worried look on her face.

"Those birds! That's what's wrong!" Mack wiped his red sweaty face with a bandana and waved his arms around. "I gotta do somethin' about 'em. Build a scarecrow, that's what."

Sally nodded. "Well, I'll help you. Come on into the kitchen for some cold lemonade and then we'll get started."

When Mack had drained his glass, he said, "I don't really have any old pants or overalls I can get rid of."

Sally thought for a minute. "That's okay. I have an old skirt and blouse we can use. And I have that old mannequin I salvaged from the department store in town when they tore it down. We'll just make a woman scarecrow."

Mack looked at her like she had lost her mind. "I never heard of such in my life, Sally Ann. A woman scarecrow?"

"Sure," she answered, nodding her head. "That'll be something those old crows won't expect."

So they drug out the mannequin from the bedroom where it had been doing its duty by posing as a sewing model for Sally. She took the dress off of it that she had been pinning up the hem on. Soon it was dressed in an old brown skirt and a white high collared blouse with ruffles down the front.

Mack looked at its flat blue eyes and straight lips that neither smiled nor frowned. "That does give me the creeps," he said, shuddering a little. "I hope it does the same for the birds!"

The mannequin had real looking black hair that Sally had drawn back in a bun. "She looks just like Mrs. Lemon, my old school-teacher," she said, giggling. "She would scare anything!"

They mounted the mannequin on a two by four that was about six feet long that Mac had found in the barn. They then attached some old work boots onto the bottom. Sally took one end and Mac took the other and they carried her to the field and set her in a hole that Mack dug with his posthole digger.

"Right in the middle, facing the road," said Mack. "That ought to take care of the birds and anyone else who comes messing around here."

They walked out to the edge of the field, and turned to look at the mannequin/scarecrow. "Wow," said Sally. "She looks so real!"

Late that afternoon Mack went back to check on his corn field. There were no birds in sight. Was it his imagination, or was the scarecrow smiling a little? 'Get a grip, Mack,' he thought. Looking around to see that Sally was not watching him, he shot the scarecrow a little salute.

The sun beat down on the scarecrow, which neither smiled nor frowned, but looked straight ahead day after day as the green corn began to grow up around it. The expressionless blue eyes continued to stare toward the road, where many a driver did a double take when they spotted the weird woman out in the field.

Mack sprayed the corn for weeds and winked at the scarecrow as he passed on the tractor. Was it his imagination or did the mannequin look longingly at him? He shook his head and laughed at himself as he continued on, up and down the rows.

The last day of spraying came and Mack was looking forward to sitting on the front porch and watching his corn grow. The cows were down in the bottoms by the river where there was plenty of good grass to eat, so he didn't have to worry about them right now. He could relax for awhile after today.

At first he didn't notice that the scarecrow was two rows closer to the house from where they had put it in the ground. When he did notice, he got mad. 'Some stupid kids, no doubt,' he thought. He wasn't thinking about how they dug another hole; he was concentrating on getting done. It didn't really matter anyway, now that the seeds had grown into plants. But the scarecrow would be useful once again when the ears developed. So he just left it there.

That night he was so tired he just left the tractor at the side of the field; the weather was fine and he could put it away in the morning.

Sally had him a good supper fixed, as usual, and later on he watched a little TV before going to bed. Sometime in the night, he awoke. He had heard something. But what? He listened hard. No sound. He glanced towards the open window by the side of his bed. Just then someone walked past the window. They went very fast, and were gone before Mack could run and look outside.

He was careful not to disturb Sally. He went out on the back porch and walked to the end next to the cornfield, which was also where his window was. He looked all around, but saw no one. Then he glanced over into the cornfield. The scarecrow was nowhere to be seen. He looked and looked for its white blouse, but saw nothing.

Mack scratched his head. That was strange. 'I'll bet whoever moved it has come back and stolen it because it was unusual,' he thought.

Just to be sure he went out and walked the fence line. 'Can't have anything in this day and time!' he thought angrily. Just in case, he walked back up the fence line to where he had last seen the scarecrow. And there it was, its profile turned away from him looking at the road like before.

Mack began to feel uneasy. Who was playing these tricks? And how had they replaced the scarecrow without his hearing them? "I wish you could talk, girl," he said to the mannequin. A breeze ruffled its clothing, making him jump. For a moment it looked like it was breathing. Mack turned and hurried back to his warm bed, but it was hours before he slept again.

He and Sally slept a little later the next morning since he didn't have anything pressing to do on the farm. He didn't tell her about his nighttime adventure. It was just too weird. And if someone was messing around with him, he didn't want to scare her.

He could not help but walk out into the corn, which was now about hip high, and look at the scarecrow. "I'll be…" he started. It was back in the original hole he and Sally had put it in. Boy, someone was going to a lot of trouble! He needed to hide out in the field tonight and find out who it was. He was perturbed. He thought of all his neighbors and who might play a joke on him like this.

They were all middle aged or older. He couldn't see any of them going to all that trouble. It had to be kids from the nearby town. They had probably seen the scarecrow as they were passing on the highway and thought it would be funny to move it around. Well, tonight he would be waiting on them.

"I sure wish you could tell me who was moving you around," he said to the scarecrow. He turned his back and began to walk away.

He heard something like , "Hmmmmm," just very soft. He turned quickly back around. No one there but the scarecrow. Had it turned slightly toward him? "Good grief, Mack!" he thought. 'You are going crazy.' He shook his head and went quickly back to the house. But the hair on the back of his neck was standing up.

By this time Sally was through with the breakfast dishes. "Mack, what is bothering you? You look worried, or something."

He tried to laugh it off. "You wouldn't believe me if I told you. It's just something silly."

She crossed her arms. "Try me."

So he found himself telling her about the moving scarecrow. "It's kids doing it, I'm almost certain. But..." he caught himself. He didn't want to tell her about the sound he'd heard that no one was there to make. No one but the scarecrow.

"I'm going to hide in the field tonight and try to catch them."

"What if they don't come back tonight?"

"Then I'll hide tomorrow night. I can't see them losing interest this quickly."

She shrugged. "Okay. You can use that old sleeping bag you used when we went camping. I'll get it down out of the top of the hall closet."

"I don't want to go to sleep."

"But you could at least sit on it and be comfortable."

Mack decided to go to town to check on winter feed for the cattle. It was never too early to make plans for the winter. Sally told him to get her a few things at the supermarket and gave him a list.

He got to talking to some old buddies he happened to run into at the co-op, so it was nearly dark by the time he got home. Expecting to smell supper cooking, he went eagerly up the back porch steps and opened the screen door. No smells greeted him, however and the kitchen was unoccupied. No lights in the house were on at all. Sally was probably on the front porch and he just didn't look that way and see her, he thought. He set the grocery bags down and went through, calling for her, but she didn't answer. She was not on the porch, either.

He was starting to get a little concerned. He went into their bedroom. There she was, in the rocking chair, her head slumped over. He started to tease her about sleeping on the job, but as he went nearer, he saw the huge gash in the top of her head and all the blood.

"Sally! Oh, what happened here? I'll call the ambulance!" he shouted, as he grabbed both her arms and began to massage them. Knowing it was far too late, he ran into the kitchen and called 911. Then he went back to the bedroom and sat on the floor by the chair.

He noticed she was wearing the new dress she had been working on before she took it off of the mannequin. The pins were still in the hem. It had blood on it. She would have to wash it once she was well. He couldn't admit to himself she was gone. He was crying and calling her name.

He heard a rustle behind him. Dreading but almost knowing what he would see, he turned to the bed. The scarecrow was lying there on its side, the quilt pulled up to its waist. Its hair was out of the bun and down around its shoulders. Its mouth had been painted red and it lay there, staring at him with its flat blue eyes.

FEAR OF FALLING

The big old house sat on a beautiful green hill overlooking the Tradewater River. Limestone cliffs rose to meet the front lawn as it sloped toward the water, and my husband Tad had built a split rail fence along the bank for safety. We often took sunset or moonlight walks, and we didn't want to inadvertently get too close to the edge.

Tad (short for Thaddeus, which he hated) Marsh had inherited the house from his grandmother when she passed away at the age of 100. He had also inherited her strength and stubbornness, which had carried her over the cliff to her death a year before we moved in, hence the fence. She insisted on "taking the air" every day, and off she would go with her sturdy walking cane wearing her sunbonnet. The protests of the various caregivers of her last years fell on deaf ears. One day she wandered too far, the bank crumbled beneath her feet, and she plummeted a hundred or more feet.

It always made me uneasy to think about it. But Tad assured me that it happened quickly; she was killed instantly when she hit the rocks below, so probably had not felt a thing. Still the fright of falling that distance must have registered as she began her descent…it gave me the willies.

After we moved in I began to have nightmares; not every night, but now and then. I dreamed I was walking along the cliff's edge and the ground gave way just behind me every time I took a step. I was walking faster and faster until I was running and short of breath. I could not seem to turn away from the edge, but was doomed to keep on until finally I was compelled to throw myself over. As with all falling dreams, I awoke the moment I lost my balance.

We modernized the kitchen and bathrooms in the house, I bought new drapes, and we ripped out the old carpet. There was beautiful oak flooring underneath. We had it sanded and stained. It was shiny and gorgeous when we were done.

I liked to run around in my sock feet and sometimes when Tad wasn't there I would slide across the hall like Tom Cruise in "Risky Business." One day I did this and my feet flew up and I fell hard on my backside. It hurt my pride worse than anything, but from then on I didn't try that any more. In fact, I stopped going in my socks and always wore shoes, or at least house slippers with a rubber sole.

I told myself I was thirty now, much too old to be acting like a teenager. You could fall anywhere, not just off the cliff, I told myself. I wondered where that thought had come from. I was not over cautious, usually. But I started to put rubber mats under throw rugs, and hold my arms out at my sides when I walked on the wood floors. One day I thought, I wonder if Tad's grandmother's old cane is still in the house. It wouldn't hurt to take it with me when I go outside.

I looked through boxes and trunks in the attic. There were many interesting things up there; antiques and vintage clothing; old toys; and laid up against a wall, the cane. I knew it was hers because I had seen a picture of her with it. I carried it downstairs and set it in the umbrella stand by the front door.

"What's this, Brenda?" asked Tad when he came home from work.

"It's your grandmother's cane. I found it in the attic when I was up there poking around," I said. Suddenly I felt foolish. Why did I bring it down here? It could not bring good things to mind for Tad.

He frowned and shrugged. "I don't know what you want it for, but okay." Then he started to tell me about his day and we went into the kitchen to start dinner and I forgot all about it.

The next morning after he left I decided I would go outside. It was such a beautiful morning. The sun was shining, the birds were singing, and the air was fresh and cool. I put on some comfortable pants and my tennis shoes and went to look out the front window. As I was crossing the hall, I tripped on something in the floor and went sprawling.

"Owww!" I yelled. My ankle had twisted as I went down. I rubbed it and rocked back and forth for a minute. What had just happened? I was always so careful. I looked around, and there lay the cane in the middle of the hall. I had fallen over it.

"How did that get there?" I was angry and a little spooked. It couldn't have jumped out of the umbrella stand all by itself. I picked it up and scooted over and replaced it in the stand. Funny. It was warm in my hand. Then I pulled myself up by holding onto a table and tested my weight on my ankle. It hurt quite a bit. I knew it would swell if I didn't get some ice on it.

I grabbed the cane and hobbled into the kitchen and fixed a plastic bag with ice and sat down with it on my ankle. So much for walking outside. I sighed. It was going to be difficult to fix dinner for Tad. Oh, well, I thought. I would just call and tell him what had happened and he could stop and get a pizza.

I left the ice on for about fifteen minutes. Then, hobbling on the cane, I made my way to the living room to turn on the TV. Walking was really painful. But I managed to get to the couch and picked up the remote. The couch was by the window that looked out toward the fence and the cliff. Someone was standing on the edge beyond the fence!

I jumped up, forgetting my ankle until it reminded me with a painful jab. Who could that be? It was a woman; she had on an ankle length dress and a scarf tied on her head. Suddenly she put her arms out and made a gesture that looked like she was warding off someone that was pushing her! But there was no one there but her. I watched in amazement and horror as she repeated the same gesture over and over, about a half dozen times. Then she seemed to just drop out of sight.

I was beside myself. I knew there was no way I could get that far. Even if my ankle had not been sprained, it would have been too late to do anything. I was certain the woman had either jumped or fallen onto the rocks below.

The phone was in the hall; I had forgotten to bring it into the living room with me. But I knew I had to call for help, so I got up and picked up the cane. Suddenly I looked at the shiny wood floor and became afraid to try to navigate it. It looked so slick. What if I fell and broke something next time? An unreasonable fear took hold of me and I couldn't bring myself to move. I knew in my head it was crazy, but I was paralyzed with fright.

Maybe I could crawl to the phone. I eased myself off the couch onto my knees and began to make my way across the floor. It seemed like a mile to the hall. I finally made it and called 911.

When the emergency squad arrived, I had managed to get to the front porch to wait for them. "A woman fell over the edge of the cliff, right behind my fence," I said breathlessly.

One of the two EMTs said, "Well, I'm sorry you had to see that. We'll go down and try to find her." It was evident in his tone that he didn't believe she would be alive. They had brought a man with them who was an experienced rock climber. He donned his climbing gear, tied his rope off at the top, and dropped over the edge.

He was gone so long I began to wonder what was going on. Finally I saw his head appear. It was obvious he had not found anything. They questioned me again about just where she had gone off. I was as baffled as they were.

After promising to mount a search party, they left. I sat on the porch a long time, not even aware of the cane in my hand. I noticed my ankle had stopped hurting. On examination I saw that the swelling was mostly gone. I tested my weight on it. Only a slight twinge remained. I was able to get down off the porch's three steps. I wanted to see the spot where the woman had gone over.

'It's all right,' I thought. 'I won't go any farther than the fence.' I made my way across the lawn to the fence and leaned over to try to see down the cliff face. The fence was far enough back that I couldn't really see anything.

I was leaning against the fence when the cane suddenly twisted in my hand and I lost my balance. I went head first over the fence, which was not quite up to my waist. I reached out to grab the fence rail and barely managed to hang on with my feet dangling over the edge. I could hear dirt and rocks falling around me. I was so frightened that I couldn't even cry out, afraid I would lose my tenuous hold on the wooden rail. There was no one to hear me anyway.

What had caused the cane to do that? I was standing still when it happened. The cane…the same one Tad's grandmother had with her when she fell. I looked at it, lying innocently on the other side of the fence. A tear slid down my cheek. I didn't know how much longer I could hang on; certainly not till it was time for Tad to come home.

There was absolutely no place for my feet to find purchase. They were dangling in midair. I tried being as still as I could. I managed to get both hands on the fence rail. I started feeling compelled to let go. It was like the dream…and I saw in my mind, almost like it was someone else's thoughts, Tad's grandmother walking along the cliff, but plenty far back from the abyss below. Then she seemed to stumble, raised her arms to balance herself, and the cane fell and became wedged between a rock and her foot. It looked like she was being pushed backward by invisible hands. Then the vision, or whatever it was, was gone and I was breathless and sweating. My hands were going numb. I knew any moment I would slip and fall. I knew then that the cane had something to do with her death, and had also caused me to fall.

Just when I thought I was going to have to let go, I heard Tad calling me. I was so weak I could barely answer. He was coming this way. I managed to let out a squawk and he began running down the lawn. "Brenda! Hang on, I'm coming to get you!"

His face was horrified when he reached over and grabbed both my arms and hauled me up and back over the fence. He hugged me to him. "Oh my gosh, how did this happen?" He was white as a sheet.

I told him the whole story once he had me back in the house, seated at the kitchen table with a hot cup of tea. "Tad, we have to get rid of that cane. I know you think I'm crazy, but please, humor me."

He nodded. "Okay," he said, not convinced but wanting me to calm down. I told him how I saw in my mind's eye how his grandmother died, with someone invisible pushing her.

"Where did she get that cane, anyway?" I asked.

"I think it was handed down through the family. Probably came over from Ireland with one of my ancestors. I mean, she didn't start using it until her older years. It was obviously handmade. No telling how old it is. She used to tell me she was so afraid of falling that she always used it, every day."

"Do you believe in ghosts?" I whispered. That was one thing we had never discussed.

He thought for a moment. Rubbing his chin, he shook his head. "I never have. But I believe you saw something; I don't know if you'd call it a ghost or what."

"I'm telling you, the woman I saw had to be your grandmother and she was trying to tell me what happened." Then I told him how I had developed an unusual fear of falling lately and it led me to use the cane. "And I'm only thirty years old. My balance has always been excellent. So why did I become so afraid? I actually have had a couple of falls, too. So I wonder if the cane had something to do with it."

"I don't know," Tad said, "but I'm going to burn the thing."

Later in the day he went out to find it where I had dropped it by the fence when it twisted in my hand. Before picking it up, he stood and looked at it awhile. Thinking he was being silly, he still did not want to touch it. So he found a long stick and pushed it over the edge of the cliff. He heard it clattering on the rocks and then nothing. Breathing a sigh, he came back to the house and told me no one else would have to worry about it causing them to fall.

Unknown to us, some people were hiking down by the river a few days later. "Look," one of them said. "An old fashioned walking stick. Wonder what happened to its owner?" And the man picked it up.

THE SNIPE HUNT

Several of my friends and I were camping out at Pennyrile State Park the weekend Dale disappeared. We had built a nice campfire and were sitting around telling stories, mostly ghost tales we had all heard a million times.

Jane, Coy, Lamont, Anna May, Hershey, and myself, Danny, had cooked it up beforehand to take our new friend Dale on a snipe hunt. Dale had moved here from Pennsylvania at the beginning of the school year. He had been hanging out with us at school. He was a pretty cool dude.

After roasting the hot dogs and making S'mores, I looked at the others and they nodded. The time had come. "Say, Dale," I asked, "have you ever tasted snipe?"

"Snipe?" asked Dale, a curious look on his face. "No, I don't think so. What is it?"

Jane piped up. "Oh, it's a bird. Delicious when roasted. They have a real tender breast meat, even better than chicken."

"Yeah, and there are lots of them right here in these woods. People catch them and roast them over their campfires all the time," I added.

"Really?" Dale's face lit up. "What do you mean, catch them? I thought people shot at birds."

"These are different. See, what you do is one person sits down and holds a bag open while the others go out and make noise and drive the snipes toward the person with the bag. They will run right into the bag." Hershey crossed his arms and grinned.

"It's pretty easy," said Coy. "In fact, I was thinking maybe we could get us some snipes tonight. So who wants to hold the bag?"

"Oh, I want to," said Jane right away.

"Or I will," said Lamont. "I don't mind."

I said, "Wait a minute. Since Dale is fairly new here, why don't we give him the easy job and all of us will go out and drive the snipes to him." Of course, we had made it up beforehand to pretend to be eager to hold the bag.

Snipe hunting is something I have only heard of in the South. A group of friends goes out into the woods, leaving one unsuspecting dope to hold the bag while they supposedly go out and shout and beat the bushes to drive the snipes in. They get further and further away, and finally, perhaps hours later, the one holding the bag realizes they aren't coming back. It's hard to fool anyone around here, as most of us have had our turn at holding the bag. Just about all kids in the South get initiated into snipe hunting sooner or later.

So Dale was fresh meat, and as innocent as a baby. I laughed to myself. I had brought along a burlap bag and soon we kicked dirt over our fire, made sure it was out, and started out through the woods. We'd gone about a mile when we came to a clearing. On one side was a rock overhang, not quite a cave, but perfect for our purposes.

"I hope I can hang onto them," said Dale. "How many do I need to catch?"

"Oh, they go in flocks, so several will probably run into the bag at the same time," Anna May said. "You'll know when to close the bag."

"Okay," I said, "we'll get started. Jane and Coy, you go out to the left, and Anna May and Lamont to the right, and me and Hershey will go straight out there. Now, beat the bushes really well, y'all!"

It was all we could do not to start laughing before we got away from poor unsuspecting Dale, sitting there under the overhang with his round, trusting face holding the bag.

So we all went our separate ways (we had agreed to meet back at our campsite) hollering and beating the bushes with sticks. We stomped the ground and went, "Snipe! Snipe! Snipe!"

The rest of the group circled around and met me and Hershey and trooped back to our camp. After having a good laugh and wondering how long it would take Dale to realize what had happened, we turned in. The girls had their tent and us guys had ours. We speculated about how mad he would be. "Oh, surely he'll forgive us," said Anna May. "He seems like a good sport."

Sometime in the wee hours of the morning I realized that I had to use the bathroom. I quietly unzipped the tent flap to step outside.

It was then I realized that Dale had not come back. I had an uneasy feeling, but talked myself out of it.

Maybe he's just paying us back by not coming in, I thought. Then I started thinking about stories I had heard about lone hikers disappearing in Pennyrile Forest. I was pretty sure they were just that...stories.

After going behind a nearby tree, I went back to the tent and nudged the nearest foot. "Hey," I said in a low voice so as not to disturb the girls. Lamont sat up, rubbing his eyes.

"It's not even daylight, man," he protested.

"I know, but Dale hasn't come back. I think we should go get him."

"He hasn't? But it's been hours!"

"Yeah. Maybe he got lost. After all, he isn't used to these woods."

Lamont crawled out from where the others were snoring. "Okay, I'll go with you. Let me grab my flashlight."

So we started off the way we had come last night. The sky had lightened considerably when we were about halfway to the rock overhang, but it was still pretty dark in the forest. It was then that we started to hear the drums. The cadence was familiar and strange all at the same time. "Hear that?" I stopped in my tracks.

Lamont was right on my heels. "Yeah. It sounds like...like..."

"Indian drums," I said. "Which is impossible, of course."

The drums continued as we started walking again. I was frightened like I'd never been before, but I didn't want to let on to Lamont. He had no such qualms.

"This is scary, Danny. Unless Dale is playing a trick on us."

"I don't think so. He didn't have a drum with him last night, now did he?"

Lamont shook his head. "No. I don't like this."

But we kept going until soon we could see the deep shadows in the rock overhang. When we got there, the burlap bag lay on the ground. But Dale was not there. We started calling his name and walking all around, fanning out a little each time.

The drums got louder, there was a crescendo, then they stopped. "There were lots of Indians around here back in the old days. Maybe someone is doing a re-what do you call it?" I said.

"A reenactment," nodded Lamont. "That has to be it. But why would they be doing it in the dark like that? And where is Dale?"

"Good question. And we need to get back and report him missing, because we're going to get lost ourselves if we keep getting further from the overhang," I said worriedly.

I was hoping against hope that Dale was just pranking us and we'd find him back at camp, his round face lit up with laughter as he told the girls that our trick had backfired. But nothing like that happened.

We had the lodge staff call the state police and Dale's parents. We found out that Iroquois had once hunted in that very area and used the rock house regularly. Did ghostly Indians carry Dale off? That was too unbelievable.

One of the maintenance guys in the lodge called me to the side while the park manager and police talked to Dale's parents. "I've heard the drums, too. Don't tell the manager. We're not supposed to talk about it. Scaring people is not good for business. But your friend will probably turn up okay. This has happened before. A guy got lost like that for three days and when he did come back he was pretty shook up. He had heard the drums and tried to find where the sound was coming from."

As I listened he told how the man came stumbling from the woods, all scratched and bloody. He had wandered in circles, the drums sometimes coming from one direction and sometimes from another. After the end of the first day, all he wanted was to find his way back to civilization. He drank from streams and picked some berries, which made him sick. At last he came across one of the park trails, and followed it to the blacktop road near the lodge.

"Did he ever find the source of the drums?"

"No. And he warned against going alone into the woods. There's something in there; Indian ghosts or whatever it might be. I know I'll steer clear of those woods. I hope your friend comes back. I've got to get to work." He left out the front door of the lodge.

"For Pete's sake!" I exclaimed to the others. "That's got to be just a story. Things like that don't happen in real life. We've got to go back up there and see if we can find Dale."

"But if the police couldn't find any trace..." began Anna May.

"We have to! It's our fault!" said Coy. "I'll go with you, Danny." I put my hand on his shoulder and nodded.

"Thanks."

Lamont and Hershey soon agreed but the girls were afraid. I told them we didn't need them and it would be a good idea if they stayed around for awhile in case Dale showed up. In the back of my mind I still was hoping against hope that he was playing a joke on us.

We started out through the woods toward the cave where we had left Dale. We didn't know where else to start. The Indians would have called it a rock house. It only went back a few feet under the cliff above.

The sky had clouded over and it was a dismal trek. It's funny how you can get spooked in a forest. You start to wonder what is hiding behind every tree. There are so many of them. And there are all kinds of sounds. Not just birds, but snaps and hollow thonks; crickets and cicadas; swishing leaves, skittering sounds like something scrambling along beside or behind you. Sometimes you can swear you hear footsteps. But when you turn around there is nothing, only the dangling leaves and the solid tree trunks, with more trees behind them, and the spaces in between blocked by brush or leaning logs covered in moss and lichen. Like it is just waiting…waiting until the time is right for something to jump out at you.

"It's like the forest is closing in around us, isn't it? Like it might swallow us." Coy's voice was shaky.

His remark so closely resembled what I was thinking that I slapped him on the back of the head before I thought. "Cut it out!

It's not alive! Well, not like that it isn't." But I was not totally convinced myself.

When we reached the rock house we began to look around for clues as to which way Dale could have gone. We found the snipe bag lying right where he had been sitting last night. I picked it up and looked inside.

Lamont said, "I doubt if he's in there." Then he looked stricken, as if the seriousness of the situation had just hit him. He wiped sweat off his forehead.

I glared at him. "I thought maybe he left a note or something." But of course, there was nothing.

A little wind had picked up, bringing the scent of rain. Soon drops began to pelt us and we were wet to the skin in no time. It was a little chilly, too.

"Man, I wish we had our raincoats," groused Coy. "We shoulda seen it was gonna rain."

"Well, we're already wet, so it doesn't matter now," said Hershey.

We found nothing on the ground around the rock house and talked about splitting up. But we were afraid to, though no one would admit it. So as a group we set out to go around the cliff to some old rock steps we knew about. They had recently been discovered by a crew that was maintaining the trail around the lake.

"Maybe Dale went up that way. Maybe he's on top of the cliff just waiting for us to find him so he can laugh at us." Hershey looked hopeful as he said this.

Somehow we didn't feel very hopeful. But we trudged on anyway. The steps were steep but not steep enough to cause any strain in climbing them. They curved around the hill to the top. By the time we got up there, the rain was a thick foggy mist that clung to everything. Looking at it, I could imagine seeing all kinds of ghosts and things.

About that time the drums started up. A slow steady thrumming with the emphasis on the first beat...BOOM boom boom boom. I jumped and so did the others. The sound of the drums seemed to be coming from all around us. We almost collided with each other as we stopped abruptly.

"Oh, no. Oh, no," said Coy. I could tell he was near panic. I was shook up myself, but tried to be calm.

"It's just a sound," I said. I remembered what the worker at the Lodge had told us and wished I was back there. Or home would be even better. But we had to find Dale. We owed it to him, because we were the cause of this predicament.

Hershey tapped me on the shoulder. "Look," he said, inclining his head towards the woods to the left of us.

I gasped as I began to see shapes in the fog. Something moving around; were they man shapes, or something else? It was almost like seeing shadows beginning to surround us. We turned in circles and the shadows were everywhere. We were huddled on the path as close as we could get to each other. Up to now the birds had been chirping and flying overhead. I became aware that every sound had stopped.

I was shivering all over, both from fright and being chilled from the rain. "Dale!" I shouted. The rest of the guys jumped.

"Shhh! You scared me out of ten years' growth," whispered Lamont.

"Dale couldn't pull this off," said Hershey as the drums grew louder.

I felt weighed down, like my legs would not move. The shapes were moving in a circle now, tightening on us like a noose. They became bigger and darker. They seemed to be flowing into one big dark thing hovering over us.

Away off in the forest a small voice called, "Here, snipe, snipe, snipe!" I almost fainted.

We were crying by now, our macho bravery the least of our worries. It got darker until we could not see. Something was pressing down on us from above, not a hard thing but a soft smothering feeling. Suddenly our legs were jerked out from under us and we all fell with a thud. We were in a bag of some kind; it felt like...it felt just like burlap.

The drums became frenzied, faster and faster and they were all around us. We heard the laughter of several men and excited voices speaking a language I didn't know. Then we felt ourselves being dragged along the path, jabbed by rocks and tree roots. We were all screaming at the top of our lungs.

Soon we were on smoother ground and I could smell smoke from a fire. Then I understood what had happened to Dale. It flashed in my mind like a movie...he must have sat there quite awhile before giving up on us. Not being from here, he didn't know his way back to the campsite. He was a city kid. Hearing the drums he decided to follow the sound. Not knowing that he was being called just like we called the snipes.

And now it was our turn.

THE GIRL WHO LOVED FISHING

"Be careful!" I shouted to my four year old daughter Layla. She was balancing on a rock in the edge of Pennyrile Lake with her Disney Princess fishing pole. I had no idea how deep it was where she was standing, but at best I didn't want her falling in and getting mud on her clothes.

"I'm careful, Mommy," she answered, looking back at me with her big blue eyes. "I'm just looking at the mermaid."

"Okay, honey," I called, getting more comfortable in my reclining lawn chair. She had one big imagination. She had decided that mermaids lived in the lake and she wanted to be one.

"Why don't you let me put another worm on your hook and see if you can catch a fish," I said.

"Oh, no, it might catch the mermaid!" She frowned at me, and turned back around and bent over to peer into the lake again.

"I think mermaids are smarter than that," I said, laughing. Layla was the light of my life, especially since my husband had died un-expectedly the year before.

She grinned and ran over to me. "Okay, Mommy, put the worm on. I love fishing!" She did a little pirouette while I baited her hook.

When I had her sitting down on the rock with her hook in the water, I settled back in my chair with my book. I kept looking up so I could keep an eye on her.

This mermaid interest had started weeks before, after we started coming to the lake at the state park to swim and fish. Layla soon became crazy about fishing and hardly ever wanted to go to the beach anymore. When she found out she could catch small fish and throw them back, she said it was the most fun she ever had.

Then she began to spend long periods leaning over and peering into the water. I would usually read, as fishing wasn't really my thing; I would hear her whispering and mumbling to herself. I had to smile. I was glad she had a big imagination and could entertain herself.

"Who are you talking to, Layla?" I asked the first time I saw her do this. She turned her head and gave me what was almost a guilty look.

"No one," she said, her eyes big and innocent. Thinking she was embarrassed at being caught talking to herself, I smiled and went back to reading. But she did this every time we came to the fishing spot now.

"Are you talking to the fish?" I asked one day.

"No, Mommy. I'm talking to the mermaid who lives in the lake. She's beautiful and I want to go down and see her."

A small chill went through me. "Little girls can't breathe in water," I said. "You can't go down in there."

She looked at me as if she was deciding if what I said was true. "Okay," she finally said, shrugging her small shoulders and picking up her pole.

"Can I see the mermaid if I come over there?" I asked.

"I don't know."

I got up and made my way to the edge of the lake. Maybe if I pretended with her, she would lose interest in going into the water. As we peered over into the wavering depths, I gave a start. Something long and pale swished back and forth in the weeds below.

'Has to be a trick of the light,' I thought. I widened my eyes to try and see more, but it was gone.

"Did you see her, Mommy? Did you see? I did!" cried Layla, hopping up and down.

"Not really. Maybe she just wants to be your special friend," I suggested.

"She wants someone to come down there. She told me she does."

This was getting to be a little creepy. "Layla, sometimes we think we see things, but we are just imagining. And that's all right, but..."

She turned her head and put her little hands on her hips. "I'm not 'magining! She's in there!" I had never seen her so angry.

I put my hand on her shoulder to pull her back from the edge. She jerked back from me and fell in. I watched in horror as my ba-

80

by sank into the weeds.

Screaming, I kicked off my sandals and dove in after her. It was deeper than I had thought. I could see Layla's wide open eyes and mouth as she sank down into the water. Finally I was able to grab her wrists. As I kicked my feet and got her in a rescue position, something rolled out of the weeds beside us.

A ghostly white face looked right at me, half eaten by fish and other creatures I didn't want to think about. Horrified, I pulled Layla to the bank and laid her out to get her breathing. Turning her on her side, I pounded her back until she coughed up the water she had breathed in. Then she began to cry.

By then several people were standing around. A lady handed me a big beach towel, which I wrapped around my daughter and hugged her tight. I could feel the tears on my cheeks as the relief that she was alive coursed through me.

"There's a body in there," I whispered as a park ranger squatted down beside me.

"In the lake?" He turned to look. As he did, the people all gasped and stepped back.

A woman's body floated face up right where Layla had been fishing a few minutes before. Layla's fall had dislodged it where it had been entangled in the weeds.

I picked Layla up and went up the hill where she couldn't see. "Did they go in to see the mermaid?" she whispered.

"It wasn't a mermaid, honey," I told her. "It was a lady who had drowned."

"No wonder she wanted someone," said Layla. "No one knew she was there."

"Yes," I said softly. "And she will be very grateful that you saw her. Now she can be buried and rest in peace." It still makes me shiver every time I think about what passed between Layla and the dead woman. I still can't quite believe it.

In the meantime,we've found a new fishing spot on Lake Beshear.

IN MEMORIAM

Ice clinked in tea glasses as the guests lingered on the long front porch of Miss Alta Brown's home not far from Gateway Cemetery, which was her final resting place. The swish of linen skirts and a slight scent of rose perfume were a balm to the senses of the folks who had come to pay their respects. Gentlemen walked into the yard to smoke cigars under the huge oak tree that had been planted by one of Miss Alta's ancestors generations before. They murmured about crop and cattle prices while the ladies on the porch went over the details of the flowers and how lovely Miss Alta had looked in her lavender suit, which her twenty-eight year old great niece had picked out and how it was a wonder it had suited her so well, since the girl had barely known her and had come all the way from Chicago to preside over the funeral and the repast afterwards. It was a pity that this girl was all that was left of Miss Alta's family.

A meal after the funeral was a tradition going back further than any of them could remember. It was not only a comfort to the soul and body, but a sign of the continuance of life for the ones left behind. Miss Alta would have wanted them to eat well. She always used to talk about how she hoped her funeral would be a celebration and not a weepy affair. It was a chance for friends and family that had not connected in awhile to visit and catch up, as well as remember their loved one.

So the ladies in her book club and friends from her church had all fixed their special dishes on their decorative egg plates and crystal platters. The thin pale-faced niece from Chicago, what was her name again... Charlotte, or Charlene or something like that...had pulled out lace tablecloths and polished silver cake forks and helped them lay out a feast that would have made Miss Alta proud.

So nice that the weather had cooperated on this day in June when sometimes the humidity could be terrible. But the sun shone and the sky was blue and a nice breeze blew across the porch. The afternoon was spent in remembrances and laughter about things Miss Alta had said and done. She had collected a lot of money for the orphans and the pregnancy care center and the building fund at the church. She kept her home as neat and spotless as she did herself; yet she always had time for a listening ear and a cup of tea.

Miss Alta had been 79 years young, as she liked to put it. She stood only five feet two, but had the commanding presence of your strictest teacher when she was trying to get her point across. Though she was soft spoken, she could be intimidating to small boys and store clerks. She had a way of looking you in the eye that made you want to stand up straight and tell the truth. On the other hand, she had the sweetest smile on her heart shaped face with a small dimple just to the left side of her mouth. Her white hair was always neatly styled in a short, waved cap. She wore silver framed glasses, which she swore she only needed for small print. Most of the time they hung on her ample bosom by a silver chain.

When Miss Alta walked down the street, her graceful hands clutching her black patent pocketbook, she never just strolled. She strode purposefully. It was clear that she had a destination; an important destination, at least to her.

The one thing she had wanted was to have her ashes scattered on the banks of nearby Pennyrile Lake, which graced the state park where she had spent so many pleasant hours of her childhood. All her friends knew this, as she had made no secret of it. But the niece, Charlotte, or Charlene....what *was* her name?! She did not believe in cremation and had had a regular funeral and Miss Alta was interred intact down the road at Gateway Cemetery, surrounded by a steel vault that would keep out a herd of elephants.

The ladies dabbed perspiration off their lips, sipped their iced tea, and whispered about how unhappy Miss Alta surely was about that. Shelly Barkman, Miss Alta's closest friend, was wiping tears with a pink lace trimmed hanky as she shook her head and lamented that it was terrible when someone's dearest deathbed wish could not be honored. (Not that Miss Alta had made the wish on her deathbed. She did not have a deathbed per se, as she had simply collapsed from a heart attack while trimming a bush in her garden).

But she had talked about it often enough that all her friends knew what she wanted.

The ladies straightened up and smoothed their hair and skirts as the niece in question approached them with a tray of cookies. Declining her ministrations with polite murmurs, they began to gather their purses and make excuses to be gone. It was nice on the porch; they had spent many happy afternoons here, visiting and embroidering with Miss Alta, or knitting socks for the war veterans. Miss Alta always said idle hands were the devil's workshop, and anyone who came to sit on the porch had something to occupy them. If they didn't bring their own work, Miss Alta usually had some beans to snap or yarn to be wound. They all sighed as they remembered, and spoke in soft voices about how they would miss her and how the town would be worse off without her and her beneficent projects. Miss Alta loved to help others, that is, the ones who couldn't help themselves. The others could go to the devil. Why, she had baked more cakes, knit more baby layettes, collected more clothing for the poor, and poured more sweet tea and lemonade at benefits than anyone in town. She didn't wait to be asked. When she saw a need, she filled it when she could. If she couldn't, she found someone who could.

Marlene (for that was her name) thanked each one of them and their husbands and brothers as they shook her hand and offered their condolences once again. She knew that underneath their southern politeness they didn't like her very much. When they had all drifted away, car doors shutting softly as if a slammed door might shatter the gentility in the air, Marlene heaved a sigh of relief. She was glad to be rid of them. Now she could do what she liked. She had inherited Aunt Alta's house, for after all, there was no other relative. She planned to sell it at the first opportunity. One thing Marlene had not inherited was her aunt's sentimentality. Maybe that came from being raised in Chicago, where life was lived at a more rapid pace.

As far as that cremation nonsense, Marlene believed in letting nature take its course. After all, Aunt Alta didn't know the difference. Funerals were for the living. And a vault had made sense to keep the grave from falling in. Marlene's parents had died years ago, and Aunt Alta was the last relative. Marlene was sure she could be forgiven for doing things her own way.

Marlene was well aware of her aunt's wishes; she had been told by the funeral director and also some of Aunt Alta's friends. She had stood firm, however. Now to pass the night in this mausoleum and put it on the market tomorrow.

The two story house was set on a large lot with mature trees and a flower and vegetable garden. Her aunt's elegant and fussy decorating style had gone out decades ago. Marlene wished she had time to change that and have the house staged to sell. But it probably didn't matter so much in the south, where time seemed to stand still to an extent. As everything was spotless and in excellent condition, Marlene didn't expect it to be on the market long.

Deep in the night she was awakened by a metallic clanging that reverberated all through the house. Sitting up in bed and rubbing the sleep from her eyes, Marlene muttered, "What the..." About that time it started again. It sounded like someone was beating the front door down with a metal rod. Or something bigger.

Sliding her feet into house slippers, Marlene switched on her bedside lamp. 3:00. Jiminy Christmas! It was pitch dark in the hallway as she negotiated her way to the top of the stairs. She wished she had a flashlight. She wasn't sure where the light switch was. As it turned out, she didn't need more light.

Moonlight flooded the hall below and reflected off the big silver object sitting in the middle of the floor. Marlene rubbed her eyes. What in the world? She was too astonished to even be frightened. She crept down the stairs, keeping an eye out for whoever might be there. Someone had to be there, for how else could Aunt Alta's vault have gotten into the house? It was certainly a vault. So it stood to reason it was hers.

"Okay, if this is your idea of a joke, it's in very poor taste!" yelled Marlene. Almost before the last word was out of her mouth, a terrific clanging started up from inside the vault. Marlene jumped and screamed.

A clump of dirt fell off at her feet. She turned and ran up the stairs and slammed and locked the bedroom door. She spent the rest of the night sitting in the middle of the bed shivering with the quilt wrapped around her. The thought that kept going around in her head was *You know Aunt Alta wanted to be cremated.* Pushing it out of her mind, Marlene watched anxiously for morning.

She did not believe in ghosts but was at a loss to explain what had happened. When the dawn crept in around the curtains she got up and cautiously went to her bedroom door. Opening it carefully, she peered into the ordinary looking hallway. *You had a bad dream. Stop being silly,* she admonished herself.

She went slowly to the top of the stairs. The hall below was clear of anything except the big grandfather clock and the umbrella stand in the corner. No vault sat there accusingly. Marlene almost grinned. Of course it had been a dream, in spite of how real it had seemed. And just to prove it she would go to the cemetery this morning and visit Aunt Alta's grave.

As Marlene drove up to the cemetery gates, a man in overalls was just opening them. He waved her on through with a nod. Of course, Aunt Alta's grave was untouched, the baskets of flowers sent by the people who had loved her still covering the whole thing. With a frown, Marlene went back to her car and climbed in. Dead people didn't know anything. They could not drag their vaults a mile up the road and slide it right in the front door. As the door appeared undamaged, someone had to have a key.

She roared off into town to the real estate office and when she had made arrangements for the agent to see the house that after-noon, treated herself to lunch at a lovely café with a courtyard full of sunshine and birdsong.

She was pleased with what the agent said she could get for the house. The lady had been in Aunt Alta's house many times and was well aware of what it was worth. Marlene expected a restful and dreamless night. It was not to be. At exactly 3:00 the clanging

started up again. Angry, Marlene determined that whoever was trying to frighten her would not succeed. She had brought a flashlight
upstairs with her and instead of turning on her bedside lamp, used
it instead. Covering the light with her hand, she made her way to
the top of the stairs. She was expecting to see who was doing this
but there was no one. Only the vault sat there, like before. The
clanging started inside and became deafening.

This time she went down the stairs and shone her light on the
vault. It was solid enough. No dream. Tentatively she laid her hand
on the cold metal. A woman's voice said, "My ashes must be scattered at Pennyrile." Marlene, startled, dropped the flashlight and it
went out. The room was very dark except for the reflection of the
silver vault.

Marlene was frightened out of her wits by now. She had been
wrong about dead people not knowing anything. "All-all right,
Aunt Alta," she said, a quaver in her voice. "I'm sorry. I'll see to
it."

Not looking back, she went up to her bedroom to spend the rest
of the night planning how to get the grave opened and make arrangements for the cremation. Downstairs, a few of Miss Alta's
closest friends, including the funeral director, wheeled the vault
out of the front door and hauled it back to the funeral home. The
director had fortunately had a key *just in case something happens,*
Miss Alta had told him as she had pressed it into his hand years
ago. "It was the least we could do," the friends agreed among
themselves. "In memoriam of Miss Alta; her wishes should not be
ignored."

THE HAUNTED PATH

A whippoorwill called in the distance as I made my way down the dark, twisted path. It was barely wide enough to walk on. Even now branches, some of them with stickers, brushed my arms as I had to turn sideways in several places. I hated the path, but I was going to be late getting home as it was. No time to go around by the road.

Mama would have supper waiting and she didn't like it when I was late. My stepfather would probably have a few words for me, too. I had had so much fun playing with my friend Carolyn that I had let the time slip up on me. Now it was almost dark.

The wind whispered in the treetops and the crickets were beginning to chirp. All was silent except for the sounds of the woods as nature settled in for the night. I could barely see two feet ahead of me and it was getting dark rapidly. My heart pounded in my chest. I had been through this path many times in the daylight, pleasantly spooked by the tales I had heard about what might be lurking there. Somehow the flying birds and the dappled sunlight just made it ordinary, and I figured the monster or whatever it was that people spoke about was just a figment of someone's imagination. I was ten years old and did not believe in that stuff anymore.

Then why was I so nervous now? It was a feeling of dread and expectation all at the same time. I tried to hurry, but the roughness of the path made it impossible. Roots tried to trip me; the thorny branches of wild blackberries caught on my clothes. The hoot of an owl made me jump. It was very different in here in the dark. A rustling off to my left...was it a deer, or a coyote stalking me, or just a field mouse? I stopped, breathing through my mouth, trying not to make any noise.

There it was again! Was it closer, or was that just my fear making it seem that way? The sweat was running down my face and my back. It had been a hot day. The treetop breeze did not seem to be making its way down low enough to do me any good, and the cloying scent of earth and old leaves almost made me choke. I began to say a Hail Mary as I felt my way along, certain that I was about to pay for every childhood transgression and sinful thought.

By now the sun was fully down and the moon had not yet risen. I wished for my Girl Scout flashlight. Of course, I had not known I would need it, for the awful path was farthest from my mind as Carolyn and I had played in the sunshine. Some night bird called and my heart almost stopped. Taking a deep breath, I told myself I needed to keep my wits about me or I would fall and hurt myself.

The path seemed to go on and on. I didn't remember it being this long. It actually cut across the field behind Carolyn's house and through a small wooded area, ten minutes at most. It seemed like I had been in here for an hour. The path had started to get steeper. It was a struggle to climb over the tangled roots.

I heard a low growl. I whimpered, and almost screamed. There it was again. Off to my left, where I had been conscious of something moments before. Scenes of sharp teeth ripping down my arms and legs filled my brain. What if it was a bear? I knew black bears had been spotted in this part of Kentucky recently. And Bigfoot was not out of the question…my imagination grew wilder and wilder. But I steered my mind away from the scariest prospect of all…a ghost or monster, something supernatural. I didn't want to go there.

I knew I had been on the path at least fifteen minutes, much longer than I should have been. I kept walking. There was nothing else to do. Periodically I would hear a growl and padding footsteps to my left, keeping pace and stopping when I stopped. I was near panic. I had to know what it was!

I looked through the bushes along the path. As dark as it was, I thought I could still make out a shadow. As I peered with great trepidation, I could make out a shape; it looked human! I raised my arms and spread them to make myself look bigger. The shadow copied my movements. "Go away!" I shouted, my voice breaking at the end. I jumped up and down. The shadow once again did the same.

"I don't know why you're scaring me, but it's not funny!" I yelled. I moved my head rapidly left, then right. My actions were mimicked exactly. So I began to have an idea. This had to be my own shadow I was seeing. But what about the growls? My mind couldn't make sense of those.

About that time, I saw two red eyes staring at me out of the thick brush and trees. They looked to be about three feet off the path and about the same height as my eyes. That was no shadow! I was so overcome that I suddenly did not care if I lived or died, just so I found out what the creature was that was stalking me.

I ran straight at it, expecting to be eaten. Instead, I felt a warmth envelop me, and a tug on my organs. It was not a pleasant feeling, but not painful either. I stopped crying and looked around. There was nothing. But my feet began to move, not as human feet, but more like a cat. I looked down and saw that I was black and covered in fur. Everything had a reddish tinge and I could see perfectly in the night. I saw far down the path, where it diverged and angled off to the right. I had the sudden urge to run as fast as I could, not out of fright, but just the sheer joy of it.

I growled...and it startled me at first. My thoughts became muddled, then about chasing prey and eating. I was compelled to run as fast as I could down the dark and twisted path, but I had no fear. I knew somehow that I would not trip and could jump high over obstacles. The thorns no longer tore at my skin, but slid smoothly through my black fur. I ran my tongue over my sharp teeth.

As I started off, I looked back and saw a dirty and disheveled child, looking dazedly about and then sinking lifelessly down onto the ground. My absorption of the child had set her free. I ran and ran, knowing eventually I would absorb another, and then it would be free as well.

THE STRANGE PLAYMATE

Callie and I were excited. Our parents were going to let us hike the Macedonia Trail by ourselves. We had done it several times with them. But at 13 years old we thought it was something we wanted to do on our own. After all, we were almost adults, for Pete's sake!

"Nancy, have you got your lunch bag?" asked Callie as she tightened the straps on her backpack. "I know how cranky you get when you're hungry." I punched her lightly on her arm.

"Of course! And Mom put some fried apple pies in. If you're nice, I might share them."

We both laughed. Callie and I had been best friends since first grade. We both loved to be outdoors in the summer. No computer or video games for us!

My dad dropped us off at the trailhead in Pennyrile Forest next to the Macedonia Cemetery. It was a perfect day, not too hot, with a nice breeze.

"You girls be careful, now, and watch for snakes," cautioned Dad. He had taught us how to tell a poisonous from a non-poisonous snake. So he wasn't too worried.

"We will, Dad! And we will meet you over at the Lodge at 4:00."

With a wave, he drove off and we plunged into the green and inviting woods. We had our walking sticks and made good use of them to hold back branches and make sure we didn't trip on the uneven ground. Leaves and other detritus covered the ground where we walked, evidence of the natural cycle of nature. We heard the calls of many birds. Crickets sang in the weeds. Once in awhile we saw a hollow log and wondered if groundhogs or other animals might have made their home inside.

The scent of pine trees filled our nostrils, along with the fine dust our feet stirred up. "A perfect June day," remarked Callie, grinning.

We had been on the trail about an hour. I said, "How about if we sit down on that log over there and have one of Mom's apple pies?"

Callie agreed at once. We each took out a bottle of water and I dug out the pies from my backpack. I looked around while we were eating, trying to identify the trees we saw. Our seventh grade science teacher had taken us on some field trips to teach us what we were seeing instead of taking everything for granted.

"Let's have a contest to see who can identify the most trees and plants!" said Callie.

"Okay. Well, there's a big water maple over there," I said pointing.

"No fair, I didn't say start yet!" she complained. She nudged me with her elbow and I almost fell off the log. Then we both started laughing.

"Okay, you go next!" I said.

By the time we finished our pies and a bottle of water each we had named over thirty different kinds of trees and plants just from where we were sitting.

"There used to be a giant oak right over there," said a voice. We both jumped.

Turning around we saw a boy about our age a little way off from behind us. "Hi!" said Callie.

"You scared us!" I said at the same time.

Instead of apologizing, he just smiled. I noticed he was half hidden behind a tree and was not coming forward. "Come on out and tell us about the oak," I coaxed. "How long ago was it there?"

I noticed there was something off about the boy and the way he kept smiling and looking at us. "I haven't talked to anyone in a long time," he said.

I frowned. "How long? An hour? A day?"

He stepped out and I was shocked to see that he was dressed in what seemed to be a deerskin outfit and some kind of high top moccasins that were laced with what looked like rawhide. He was very pale and bony. There was something about him that made him seem not quite all there. I don't mean in the head; I mean he didn't look clear. I rubbed my eyes; there must have been a film over them.

"Oh, a lot longer than that," he answered. "It has taken me over two hundred years to learn how."

Callie and I laughed and looked at each other. "May as well play along," I said out of the side of my mouth. She nodded.

"Who made your outfit?" I asked. "It looks really authentic."

He looked amazed at my question. "I made it myself, with my father's help. We tan our hides and cut our own rawhide and it takes a long time to make one. But they last for years. That is, I have outgrown a few and have to have them more often."

He cocked his head on one side. "I have to say I have never seen clothes like yours." We looked down at our T-shirts and jeans. This was starting to feel creepy.

He came a little closer. He looked more substantial up close. "I got an idea! Why don't we play some games! I know a good one. It's called Hop, Step, Jump."

"Well, we have to finish the trail before 4:00," said Callie. "Nancy's dad is picking us up in his SUV."

"SUV? What on earth is that?" The boy looked genuinely puzzled.

"A car," said Callie, frowning.

"I don't know what that is. But the game won't take very long. Here's how it goes: each person takes a hop on one leg; then a long step, then a long jump. The one who goes the farthest is the winner."

"Are you serious?" I asked. I wanted to say I had never heard of anything so silly, but having been taught politeness, I didn't.

He demonstrated the game to us, and as we saw no harm in it, we laid down our packs and followed his instructions, not noticing that each hop, step,and jump took us deeper into the woods and away from the trail. It was easy to get caught up in it. Soon we were all three laughing like hyenas, especially when I took a fall on my backside and got dirty.

"What's your name?" I finally thought to ask. He was way ahead of both of us, even though we had all started at the same place.

"John. What's yours?"

"I'm Nancy, and this is Callie," I answered.

"Do you live around here?" asked Callie. I had begun to think maybe he didn't live at all, but kept that to myself, along with the idea that I might be going crazy.

"What's your last name?" she asked before he could answer the other question. He never did answer that question, but supplied his last name.

"Salling. John Peter Salling the second."

"I've never heard that name before," she said, taking another jump.

"My father is an explorer. He and some other men and I started out from Virginia earlier this year to explore all the way to the Mississippi River. John Howard was our leader. He promised each man 10,000 acres of land if we made it all the way to the Mississippi. But then we were attacked here by Indians. There must have been a hundred of them. It was awful."

The boy looked pained. By this time Callie and I were baffled and a little frightened.

Our mouths dropped open as he described the fight with the Indians, and how a tomahawk thrown by one of the braves had split his head open. "I fell right there," he said, and pointed at a spot a few feet ahead. "I never did know what happened to Father and the others. It sure has been lonely out here. I'm glad to have playmates." And he grinned. This time it didn't look quite so friendly.

My hair was standing on end. I looked around us. I had no idea where we were or how far we had come from the trail. "Callie…"

I turned to look at her, and saw the horror on her face. Looking back at the boy, I saw that his head had a huge bloody gash in it and the blood was running into his eyes. He fell down on the ground and disappeared.

We were too horrified to talk as we turned round and round looking for the way back to the trail. We were crying by now and frightened out of our wits. "Calm down," I said as much to myself as to Callie.

"I've got my phone," I said, "we can look at the GPS." Then I remembered that it was in my backpack lying beside Callie's on the log.

"I guess you know we don't have anything," she said, between sobs.

"We can watch the sun! When it starts going down we can tell which direction to go. The trail runs from east to west. So all we have to do is go north with the sun on our left and we should come to the trail."

She looked at her watch. "But it's already 3:00! We'll never make it before dark."

"When we don't come out of the woods, I mean, *if* we don't, Dad will mount a search party. It'll be okay."

We sat down on the ground a little ways from where the boy had disappeared. I thought about and wondered whether the men were all killed or if they buried him, or had to leave him. It was a morbid train of thought. I determined to look up that name in a Kentucky history book as soon as I got home.

Soon we could see the sun was lower in the sky, and started walking. We were back on the trail by 4:00 and it took us until right at dark to get to the lodge. My dad was just getting ready to call out the state police and their search dogs when we came in. His worry turned to anger. He was mad as hops.

"The first time I trust you girls to go hiking on your own, and this is what you do! What have you got to say for yourselves?"

We looked at each other. We knew we couldn't tell him the truth. "Well, we started playing this old pioneer game," I said.

IN THE FOG

David steered carefully around a sharp curve in the driving rain. He glanced over at his sleeping wife Donna. Her head was leaned over against the passenger side window, mouth open. If the rain wasn't so loud, he could probably hear her snoring.

They were headed into Pennyrile Forest for a much needed September weekend getaway. Both had extremely busy careers. They were looking for a peaceful place to unwind. Several of their friends in Lexington had recommended Pennyrile for its lodge with all amenities, along with activities like hiking, swimming, and golf. Donna and David were only interested in sitting and watching the wildlife and spending some time together.

Now the rain seemed to be spoiling their weekend. It was not forecasted, but had seemingly sprung up out of nowhere. And they had left Lexington much later than planned. It was already almost dark, which didn't help the visibility. Once he turned off the main highway, the road was so crooked that David began to wonder if a drunk had laid it out.

Oh, well, he thought, we can cuddle by the large fireplace his friends had described. Perhaps enjoy some hot cocoa and read some books. He was determined not to let the wet weather ruin their good time. Friday night was shot, but there was always hope for the next two days.

The tires swished on the wet pavement in a rhythm that was hypnotic. And besides that he saw that a fog was starting to roll in. Great! He slowed down even more as the mist began to swirl. How much farther could the Lodge road possibly be? It seemed like he had been on this road for hours. In reality it could not have been more than a few minutes.

As the fog intensified, the rain began to lessen. David cracked his window to get a little air. It was refreshing. The rain had cooled things off. A light pine scent floated in on the air. There were more curves. The road was very narrow. He concentrated on the few feet he could see in front of the car.

Donna finally woke up, rubbed her eyes, and stretched. "Where are we?" she croaked, her throat dry from sleeping with her mouth open. She reached for her bottle of water in the cup holder.

"Almost there," said David. "It's been raining quite hard. So I'm taking it slow."

"I didn't even hear it. I must have been really tired." She peered through the windshield. "My goodness, it's foggy!"

David didn't answer. Had he seen lights coming toward them? Or was it his own headlights reflecting back at him through the heavy fog? He strained to see. But the visibility was only a few feet in front of the car. "I'd pull over, but the shoulder is kind of a drop-off. And we'd be sitting ducks if another car came up from behind."

Donna sat up straighter and said, "This is so creepy. How much further is it?"

"I don't know!" David snapped back. "You know I've never been here before."

"Funny," Donna said dreamily. "I feel like I *have* been here before."

David took his eyes off the road for a moment. That was such a strange statement for her to make. When he looked back, two bright headlights were coming right at them.

There was no time to react before the crash. As David lay dying, he reached out to his wife and took her cold hand in his. He suddenly had the same sense of déjà vu she had had.

The older couple in the other car slid to a stop in the middle of the road. The man fought to keep his car under control. They both sat shaking as they tried to get their wits back. The seatbelts had held them when the man stamped violently on his brakes.

He jumped out of his car. Looking all around, all he saw was the swirling fog. He had definitely hit the other car, but heard no sound. Its lights had vanished off the side of the road. He ran to the edge of the road and looked into the bushes. It was so dark he couldn't tell a thing about what was there. But he didn't see anything. He looked at his own front bumper and saw no damage.

He got back into the car, and his wife looked at him questioningly. He shook his head. Then he drove up to the cemetery a little way up the road and turned around. They had had dinner at the restaurant at the lodge and were on their way home. But the man knew he had to report the accident, even though there was nothing there.

Back at the lodge, they were given hot chocolate and led to the fire. The desk clerk gave them blankets because they were both shivering. "It happens now and then," he said. "There was a young couple killed in a head-on collision there about twenty years ago on a foggy night like this one. You are not the first ones who have seen it happen again."

EYES

I won't tell you that I am brave but I also won't tell you that I am easily frightened, or believe in spirits, or anything like that. My grandpappy taught me that if you see something at night that looks ghostly, just go up and touch it and it will turn out to be something ordinary, like a coat hanging up or a sheet flapping on a clothesline. But there was this one time...

Lick Creek Cemetery is in the Pennyrile region of Kentucky, just off a state highway on a road that loops back onto another highway. I have relatives buried there and so do a lot of other people I know. It has always been reputed to be haunted, even when Lick Creek Church was still standing, even though by the time I learned about it the church had been long abandoned. Its empty windows and door gaped darkly from the hill on which it stood. As teenagers, we used to drive by there at night and recall all the stories that had been told to us by various people, most of whom could not be believed. But as young people do, we liked to scare ourselves. It became a sport for boys to take their girlfriends out there to see if they could scare the girls into letting them put their arms around them.

I had just gotten my driver's license. One night my dad let me drive the car, supposedly to the Dairy Maid to get some ice cream with a couple of my friends, Peck and Charlie.

"Now, Stevie, you be sure and don't go nowhere else," he said gravely, handing me the keys.

I solemnly promised, even though I had crossed two fingers behind my back.

Because the truth was, we planned to pick up the girls we liked and take them to Lick Creek. I had a crush on Mary Alice, a fifteen year old a year behind me in school. I had asked her if she would like to go get ice cream that evening. I was thrilled when she said yes. Charlie's girl, Sara Ellen, thought we were going to just cruise the town. Peck didn't have a girl yet, though he was looking. He was a little shy.

When we told him our plan, and asked if he would help us scare the girls, he readily agreed. But when we told him it involved taking him to Lick Creek Church and dropping him off and leaving him while we went to town to pick them up, he wasn't so excited. "Y'all know how creepy that place is," he said, looking worried.

"Yeah, but you won't be there long. Besides, you know there's no such thing as ghosts," I said. Of course, I knew he would not admit it if he did.

He finally agreed. When we drove up to the church that September night about 6:00, it wasn't quite dark, so it didn't look all that scary. We had brought a lawn chair for Peck to sit in, and

Charlie had filched a white sheet from his mama's linen closet for him to put over himself when he heard our car. By this time we were all laughing about how much fun we would have.

"Now sit right in the doorway," instructed Charlie. "And when we drive up, jump up and start waving and going 'Boooooo!' Peck agreed and we drove away as he was adjusting his sheet and getting comfortable.

Mary Alice and Sara were not too keen when we told them we were going someplace else before we got ice cream. But we convinced them and about 45 minutes later, we were on the road to Lick Creek.

"I know where we're going," said Sara from the back seat. "Lick Creek! I hope we don't see a ghost," she said. I could tell she wasn't really scared, though.

"I don't want to go out there," said Mary Alice in a very small voice. She scooted across the seat next to me, which was just fine.

"I'll protect you, Mary Alice," I said in my most manly voice. "No ghost can get near you; I'll see to that."

"I've heard that people see eyes in that cemetery," she said. "They move all around. Have you seen it, Steve?"

I had to admit that I had not, but had heard about it. "We're going to see for ourselves," I promised. "I'll bet it's not ghosts at all." Secretly I was laughing inside at the thought of what the girls would do when they saw Peck in the doorway.

The clearing in front of the church became visible on the right, and we turned off and started up the hill. It was full dark. The moon was out, but it was only a half moon, so it didn't give much light. I had to admit the old white building did look ghostly, rearing up in our headlights.

"Look!" shouted Mary Alice.

I could see Peck in the doorway, swaying as if in a wind. This was better than I had imagined. "Oh, my gosh! A ghost!" I tried to sound convincing.

Sara was straining to look over the back seat. "That isn't real! I know you guys! You set this whole thing up!"

I was a little disappointed that she had figured it out so quickly, but wasn't going to give up yet. "No! Honest," I said, trying to put a little tremor in my voice. "I'm not going any farther."

Then I looked out my side window toward the cemetery. There were glowing eyes everywhere! I gasped. Mary Alice was right! I said an ugly word, drawing a sock on the arm from Mary Alice.

Charlie said, "Let's get out and go see what it is."

"No," I said. "I'm not going out there." I was regretting the whole thing. And Peck was still in the door doing his thing; only it seemed that he had grown taller. He must be standing in the lawn chair. Surely not, the thing would collapse.

"Let's get out of here," whimpered Sara. "I know you couldn't have set up those eyes. They are going to come after us any minute!"

About that time, Charlie opened his door. "What are you doing!" I was panicked.

"I'm going to confront the ghost in the door," he said calmly.

"What about the eyes?" said Sara.

I saw Charlie hesitate. "Has to be some kind of animals," he said confidently.

I was amazed that Peck didn't come running to the car, afraid of all the eyes. Then I realized he couldn't see them from his angle. He could only see straight out the door.

I also didn't believe that many animals would be all together in a cemetery at night. I knew what Grandpappy had told me, but I was shaking all over. I was sure he had never seen anything like this. Mary Alice was clinging to my arm, which ordinarily would have been very pleasant.

I leaned out my open window. "Peck! Get in the car! I'm leaving!"

"I might have known!" screeched Mary Alice. "All a trick!" She jumped out her passenger door and started running up to the church.

I saw the ghost in the door and then I didn't. It was like Peck had just vanished. Charlie followed Mary Alice, and then Sara got out of the car. Reluctantly, keeping an eye on the cemetery, where the eyes were moving all over the place, I went after them. I had a bad feeling.

"Peck! Come out!" shouted Mary Alice. "We know it's you!"

But there was no answer, only the moaning of the wind through the empty windows. The church was empty. "Okay, this is too spooky," whispered Sara.

"Yeah, where could he be?" asked Charlie.

"We're going to have to look for him, and when I find him, I'll…" I began.

About that time we were going back outside when there was a moan from the cemetery. We stopped in our tracks.

"Did you hear that?" said Sara.

I really did not want to go into that cemetery. And the others didn't, either. We all drew close together in a huddle. "Maybe Peck is trying to scare us," I ventured.

"But he couldn't make those eyes appear," said Mary Alice. "Something must have happened to him." And she began to cry. I hate it when girls cry.

I knew we had to investigate. "He might be hurt," I said. "I don't know why he'd go into the cemetery, though."

I got my flashlight from the car and we made our way towards the cemetery, and all the eyes suddenly disappeared. But we heard the moan again. The wind was still blowing and the trees whispered as if to say, Beware!

I got a little braver after the eyes were gone. I agreed with Charlie that it had to be animals. Soon we came upon Peck lying on the ground. Just as we came up to him, he sat up and screamed.

I grabbed his arms. "It's just us, you dolt! What happened?"

He put his hand on his head and I could see that the side of his head was bleeding.

"There was a real ghost in the church!" he said. "I'm not lying! It was white just like me! Only it was a lot taller. It was floating toward me. So I ran. I tripped on a root or something and hit my head when I fell. That's all I remember."

I got goosebumps all over me. It wasn't Peck in the church when we drove up. That was why the ghost looked taller.

"Weren't you afraid of the eyes in the cemetery?" asked Sara.

"What eyes?" said Peck. "Oh, yeah. I did see those. They scattered and ran when I started up here. At the time the ghost was scarier."

About that time, we heard a "meow" from somewhere. And a set of eyes appeared not a foot from where we stood. We all began to laugh. Helping Peck up, laughing like hyenas, we momentarily forgot about what we had all seen in the church. Relief made us giddy, I guess.

"They must come up here to catch field mice," I said. "Cats! That's all it was!"

Peck was laughing by now, too, so we knew he wasn't seriously hurt. "But what about the other ghost? I mean, the white one."

"Oh!" Mary Alice said. I looked and she pointed towards my car. A great white misty cloud hung in front of it, right at the driver's door.

We all huddled close together again wondering what to do. "It's just fog," I whispered. But I wasn't sure. About that time we heard a sound like the clanking of chains. We all jumped at the same time.

I don't know how long we stood there, but finally the fog began to dissipate and was soon gone. I suddenly became aware of crickets in the grass and the hoot of an owl. Cicadas sang and twigs snapped.

"I think we've seen enough," said Peck. "I don't really care about coming here again. And let me tell you, it was plenty spooky up here even before I saw the ghost."

We didn't correct him on the "ghost" part. After all, I'm sure my grandpappy didn't know everything.

ABOUT THE AUTHOR

Rebecca Solomon lives with her husband, Mark, and their spoiled cat, Ana, in western Kentucky. She enjoys reading, scrapbooking, and volunteering.

Made in the USA
Columbia, SC
14 October 2017